The Returning

Beca Lewis

PERCEPTION PUBLISHING

Contents

Forward

It's a funny thing about comin' home. Looks the same, smells the same, feels the same. You'll realize what's changed is you. — F. Scott Fitzgerald

One

If it were possible to move as slowly as a sloth, Serenity Rivers was accomplishing it. But she wasn't proud of it. How could she have let this happen?

The predawn bird chorus was singing so loudly she could barely hear herself as she berated herself for being so out of shape. Were they mocking her? She wouldn't blame them. This was all her fault.

Every step was a struggle. Her knees ached and her hips hurt. But it had to be done. Being a sloth was not an option anymore because now simply walking what would be only a few blocks if she was in a town was so hard she wanted to sit down and cry. She yearned to stop. Perhaps sit down and enjoy the sensations of being in nature. Pretend that she didn't hurt all over. Listen to the birds sing and watch the wind flip the leaves on the trees.

But even though it was unlikely that a car would pass here so early in the morning, she still was not going to allow herself to stop now. If she sat down, she was afraid she wouldn't be able to get up again. So she walked and tried not to moan with each step.

As she took one step forward at a time, Serenity knew she needed to stop the bad self-talk. It's how she got here in the first place. She had fallen into the habit of beating herself up for everything she was afraid to do and was hiding from. But then, it was so much easier to spend time alone. Once her paintings had started to sell, she only had to deal with a few people, and as time went on, she had isolated herself more and more.

Living within her imagination was wonderful, but it had been a mistake to think that she could forget the rest of the world. And it was definitely wrong to forget that she was human and needed to take care of herself.

Even now, in the state she had let herself fall into, Serenity tried to rationalize that she had valid reasons for her choice. But with each step, harder than the last one, Serenity knew she had been wrong.

She had to admit to herself that she had made a mistake. Her cowardice had led to laziness and self-pity. If she went anywhere, she drove, never walking, for heaven's sake. She might see someone and have to talk to them. Which meant that now, in the middle of her life, she found herself in this predicament, barely able to walk down a country road without groaning with each step.

However, despite how much she was tempted to continue berating herself, Serenity knew that being mad at herself for what she had done and where she was now wouldn't help.

Acknowledge it and move on, she said to herself. It was time to put on her big girl pants and grow up. She couldn't afford to be a coward or lazy anymore. Her mother needed her. And like all the dutiful daughters of all the Rivers women before her, she had answered the call and had returned home.

She supposed someday her daughter, Samantha, would come home to care for her as she lay dying, but that better be a long time in the future. And it was also possible Sam wouldn't come. Sam just might choose to let her mother die alone, and Serenity knew she wouldn't blame her for that choice. Why should daughters have to come home to care for their mothers?

In fact, it was entirely possible Serenity wouldn't tell her daughter she was dying. She would free her from the responsibility and let her break from the tradition of daughters caring for mothers. As Serenity walked, she allowed her thoughts to drift to her daughter. It had been a few years since she had seen her. They texted occasionally and even less often spoke on the phone. Each time they spoke, Serenity imagined what Sam looked like now.

That wasn't hard to do. She could simply look in the mirror and see herself twenty years younger. Just as she could look at her mother and see herself twenty years in the future. All Rivers women looked alike. If time stopped and they were lined up in a row at the same age, it would be hard to tell them apart. Except for the color of their eyes and hair.

Her daughter Samantha had eyes the color of dark green moss and long shiny dark straight hair that Serenity had spent many hours brushing as they laughed and sang together. But that had been years ago. It had been a long time since they had laughed and sang together.

Serenity's eyes were a startling shade of blue, a blue that contrasted with her bright red hair and made people look twice, which had never made her happy. She had always wanted to fade into the background and had tried dying her hair and wearing contacts. But in the end, she opted to stay out of sight as much as possible instead.

People said beauty was a gift, but it was also a burden. Just one more burden that the Rivers women had to bear. It was not something they could change, just as they couldn't change the other gift that they shared.

Even as frail as she was, Elizabeth, Serenity's mother, was still beautiful. Yesterday, when she saw her, Elizabeth's long white hair was spread out on her pillow-framing eyes that were still a deep shade of blue that was almost purple. If there was such a thing as having purple eyes, then that's what Lizzy had.

When Serenity had stepped up to her mother's bed, having driven ten hours to be there, Elizabeth had smiled, reached out and held Serenity's hand, and thanked her for coming. *As if I could refuse*, Serenity had thought. Holding her mother's hand, a pang of guilt had run through her. She should have come sooner. She should have stayed home instead of leaving her mother alone all these years. She should have not been such a coward. So many shoulds.

But it was not just her fault. Her mother had never once asked her to stay, and then once she was gone, neither one of them had reached out to the other. Both of them were retreating from life, unwilling to deal with the burden of what people called a gift.

But it wasn't a gift if it meant you spent your entire life hiding from it. From the power of it. But her mother had, and she had followed in her footsteps, and her daughter in hers.

It was going to have to be Serenity that accepted the gift and used it. Her mother had confirmed it for her last night.

As Serenity held her mother's hand, Lizzy had taken deep breaths and told Serenity that she had been wrong. Their gift of seeing other people's memories was to be used, and Serenity would have to be the one to figure out how to change generations of hiding and to use their gift for good.

"No," Serenity had replied. "Not me."

Her mother, appearing as frail as someone could be and still be alive, had pierced her with a look that had drilled into her soul and said, "Yes. You. And Samantha."

Which is why she was out walking at 5:00 in the morning, down a back road lined with trees, with hay fields in between, trying as hard as she could to avoid people as she always had. As with every Rivers woman, every person could be dangerous to her because they could trigger the so-called gift and send Serenity into their world of memories.

Serenity thought about the first time that had happened to her. It had brought her to her knees as if someone had punched her. She had run home to her mother crying, her red hair tangled in the tears on her face.

Elizabeth had taken one look at her and knew. Wrapping her arms around her, she had whispered, "It's a gift, Serenity."

It didn't feel like one.

Two

L izzy lay in bed watching the breeze blow through the white gauzy curtains, sending fluffs of white into the air like clouds. She always left a window open at night, needing to know there was fresh air coming into the bedroom.

A small shell-shaped nightlight highlighted the door. Its light threw shadows on the wall and caught the edge of the curtains as they puffed out, making ripples of light in the dark.

Sometime in the night, Serenity must have checked on her because the quilt her mother made that had been at the foot of the bed was now covering her. Her eyes misted at the care. She would have been cold this morning. June temperatures often dropped quickly in the night, only to rise later into a heatwave.

Everything seemed so out of balance to Lizzy. Thinking about the past, it seemed the weather was more consistent then. But not necessarily. She knew as well as anyone that what you remembered was probably not exactly what happened. Both the present and the future colored the past.

Since she knew that time is fluid, she had often wondered if when she remembered something, it actually changed the past or just her memory of it. And if that altered memory changed the past, would it change her future self? But then, how would you know? Maybe it happened all the time. With fluid time and many dimensions, anything was possible.

Lizzy shut her eyes, squeezed them tight, and told herself to stop thinking that way. It could lead to craziness. Best to deal with what was in front of her. There was plenty to handle; she didn't need to let her imagination run wild. Maybe it was only possible to live in the moment, anyway.

And at this moment, there were many things to deal with. One was the possibility of her impending death. Of course, death was always impending, but in this case, if something didn't change, she could see it coming straight towards her. Sometimes she could see death hanging around in the corner of the room, smiling at her.

But it was giving her time to make things right, and she was going to use that time well. And then she'd let herself float back into the river of time and let it take her elsewhere. Until then, she had work to do.

The back door opened and softly closed. Glancing at the clock by her bed, Lizzy saw it was just 5:00 in the morning. She smiled to herself. She had been right. Serenity was making a choice to stop hiding. It was possible that she could help Serenity be the one to bring back the gift and use it well.

All she had to do was stay alive long enough to help her do it. And maybe repair the rift between Serenity and Samantha. Separations and rifts were not the way the Rivers women used to be. They stayed together and made a difference.

Long lines of women had lived in this same house, watching the comings and goings of each of them. Cuddling the new ones, holding hands as the old ones moved on. Sometimes Lizzy thought she could hear them whisper together, but she knew that was her imagination. Wishful thinking. None of them would stay around. they would all slide gracefully to the next place, wherever that was. Earth and humans were hard on them, and they would be grateful for the respite. As she would be.

But she would hold off as long as she could. Repairs had to be made to the line of Rivers women. And since she was the one who had broken them, she would have to be the one who repaired them. Breaking them had not been intentional, but repairing them would be.

For a moment, Lizzy wondered if her illness wasn't real. Perhaps it had happened so that she would break down and reach out to Serenity. If she repaired what she had broken, would she become well? Would death step away for a while and let her enjoy life with her daughter and granddaughter for a little longer?

Although it was a possibility, she couldn't think about that. This was not about her. *For once,* she muttered. She knew she was being hard on herself; everyone made their own choices. She hadn't been alone in making the break.

While she waited for Serenity to return, she let herself drift in and out of sleep, remembering her past and the events that had led to the rift between the last of the Rivers women. Last, because Sam showed no signs of caring about carrying on the tradition of one man, one child—always a daughter.

The tradition had also always included that all Rivers women lived without a man. They could have one in order to have a child. But once they accomplished that, he had to leave. They were like some spiders. Find a mate and then get rid of them. Except they didn't eat them. Just pushed them away.

Now, lying in bed, reliving her life and determined to break this cycle, Lizzy let herself regret that tradition. Who started it anyway? Why couldn't they have long-term relationships and feel loved their entire life? Raise a normal family? Even after all these years, she could feel the yearning for Matthew, her man. What would her life have been like if she had let him stay? What would Serenity's or Sam's life be like?

But would Matthew have been able to tolerate what she could do? Would she have been able to stop the seeping in of his memories into her thoughts? Or if she saw them, would she be able to let them go and not let them color her reactions or feelings? Was it possible? And because she wasn't sure that it was, Lizzy sighed, thinking that perhaps they had been right to choose to live alone. She knew what people thought about the Rivers women being able to see all their memories. All their memories. From the time they were born, and sometimes before.

Not all at once. They seeped in. At the most inappropriate times.

The first time Matthew kissed her, he remembered his first kiss. And that was the kiss he remembered as the best kiss. Not hers. A girl with short, curly brown hair and a beautiful smile lived on as his perfect kiss. Yes, a normal person might have told about that memory, and it might have still hurt a tiny bit knowing you weren't the one. But seeing his memory, she felt all that he had felt and knew she would never live up to it.

It had broken her heart even before they had a chance to fall in love. Which she had done. And she had done her best to close herself off to all his memories. Even his memories of her as they lay in bed together. Despite that, it was impossible to not love him and his kindness and gentle ways. He had passed on his blue eyes and red hair to Serenity. But he didn't know that. She had pushed him out of her life as soon as she knew she was pregnant. That was the way it worked.

But now, Lizzy wondered if there was another way. Could they tame the gift, keep it, but only use it if and when it was needed and the rest of the time live like normal people?

That's what she wanted to know and was determined to find out. She wanted to give Serenity and then Samantha a gift. The gift of freedom.

It was time for Rivers women to be free. And she would figure out how to do that. Even if it killed her. And given her current condition, it just might.

Three

Serenity glanced at her phone and saw that she had walked, struggling, an entire half mile. It was time to turn around and return. The way she felt made her think she shouldn't have walked so far. What if she never made it back? It would be humiliating to call an Uber to take her only a half mile.

Even though she wished she hadn't walked so far, she knew why she had done it. Walking used to be easy. Taking a break between paintings, she'd walk out the door and walk for miles before turning around. And that was in the mountains, where the walking was up and down.

She knew why she had stopped taking daily walks. She could claim laziness, like any normal person would, but in her case, it was more than that. First, the trails had gotten busier. That in itself wasn't pleasant. She had enjoyed the quiet and solitude, but as the years went by, no matter what time of day she went, someone else would be there.

Too often, they didn't respect the gift of nature. They'd be on their phones talking too loudly. Or they'd be wearing ear buds listening to something so they couldn't possibly be hearing the bird songs or quiet movements of the animals through the brush. All of which annoyed her, even though she knew it was their right to be oblivious.

If there was more than one person, too often, they'd be talking loudly as if they were in a crowded room and needed to be heard instead of being under the dome of a beautiful, ever-changing sky with towering trees and gentle winds.

You are missing everything, she'd want to say to them. But that conversation couldn't happen. Who knew how they'd react? And besides, that simple exchange could open the door to their memories, and that would be an invasion of privacy for them and painful for her.

Instead, it was best to be as invisible to them as possible, her red hair tucked up into a cap and sunglasses over her impossibly blue eyes. Over time, the walks became less and less pleasant until she finally stayed home and sat in the backyard and enjoyed nature there instead.

She told herself that she didn't need to walk to see anything. The sky, the trees, the birds, and the animals could all be enjoyed at home. So she sat and took it all in. It was safer. But that decision turned her legs into mush. She gained weight and grew soft and lazy.

She was paying the price now, huffing loudly, pausing, catching her breath, and then limped along. Despite the pain, Serenity was happy that she was finally doing something about her health and even happier that she hadn't seen anyone along the road this morning that might remember her. Only one car had passed her on their way into town, but they had barely glanced her way, and she had been careful to not focus on them just in case that might open the door to a memory.

Fifteen minutes later, she had stepped off the road onto the long lane to the Rivers House. That was what everyone called it. Some people thought it was because a river ran through the property in front of the house. And some people thought it was because Rivers women lived there. *Either was correct*, she supposed.

In fact, it was entirely possible their last name was Rivers because of the river. It was something she might try to find out. The normal way. Not looking into someone's memories. Besides, there was probably no one still alive who knew the answer.

The lane was rutted and uncared for. She knew her mother had intentionally kept it that way so people would not feel it was necessary to drive down it. But the postman and delivery people had become increasingly unhappy about the drive and threatened to stop delivering unless something was done about it.

As she carefully picked her way around the ruts and stones, Serenity agreed with them. Something had to be done about it. And the house. Just one night in the house had been enough to realize how badly it had been neglected. Just like herself and just like the Rivers gift. All neglected for the same reason.

Today, she would start the process of finding someone to help with the house and drive. The only other choice was to take her mother away from all of this. And that was something she knew couldn't happen. This was where they belonged.

She hadn't told her mother that she had decided to sell her house in the mountains and move home permanently, but she assumed Lizzy knew. Not because she read her memories, but because she knew her daughter. Lizzy would know she would feel obligated, as all of River's daughters did. Maybe even hers.

She had called Samantha as she drove to Lazy Rivers and told her about her grandmother's illness. Sam had said she'd be there. When she wasn't sure. Serenity had felt a jolt of happiness at the possibility of seeing her daughter. Even if it was only because her grandmother was sick.

As for the house, there was so much work to be done. She had already packed up her own house, knowing long before Lizzy called that the time was coming to move home. All the paintings she had finished and was storing at home were now headed off to her agent. The unfinished ones were on the way to the town of Lazy Rivers.

Not that she wanted to move home. She just knew it was what had to be done. And it wasn't just about coming home to take care of her mother. Something else had been calling her. It wasn't exactly a memory, at least not the kind that was like watching a movie. No, it was like a lingering thought in the back of her head. A memory, yes, but not clear enough to be seen. Something she knew but couldn't remember, and it was here in Lazy Rivers that it would be resolved.

Many years before, someone planted rows of poplar trees along the lane to the house. Vines and weeds grew up around them now. The lane took one last curve and the Rivers house was in front of her. Rebuilt after a fire in the early 1900s, it looked every bit its age. The front porch tilted, some siding had fallen off, and the windows were so dirty with age that there was no need for curtains.

Her designer eye was already remodeling the house, not just fixing it. She was sure her mother would agree. Anything to have her daughter home. The problem would be dealing with the workmen and their memories that would invade their space. But something had to be done.

As Serenity pulled herself up the rickety steps to the front door, she imagined the day that it would be easy. Perhaps she'd look back on the year as the year of renovation—for herself, the house, and perhaps even her family.

But there was still something else going on. The lurking thought in the back of her mind was that she had forgotten something important. And despite her efforts to keep from feeling anything, she knew there was something that had happened recently in town that the town needed her to remember.

As much as she didn't want to, she knew she would. Obligation was her middle name. Or had been before, and was now again.

Four

It was a long drive, something Samantha was grateful for. She needed time to think. Why was she doing this? She hadn't seen her grandmother for almost twenty years. Her mother for almost ten. What was wrong with her family, anyway?

It was a moot question. She knew what was wrong with it. It was why she had to take the long and winding way to get to the house where Rivers women lived. Avoiding highways and busy intersections. Traveling every backroad she could find. Her GPS had to keep adjusting as she took what she supposed it would think was the scenic route. Fewer homes. Fewer cars. Fewer people meant that there was less chance she would be slammed into a memory.

Not hers. Theirs. She hated it. If she could carve that part of her brain away, she would gladly yield to a surgeon's knife. In every other way, she was normal. And there were long stretches of her life when the "gift" faded into the background and let her be. She could make friends and hang out with them like a regular person. She'd have to wait until they told her something before she would know it.

But she didn't really want to know anything. She was afraid of their secrets and refused to listen to them when they tried to tell her. Sam knew that any secret could flip open the door to seeing memories, and then everything would change. She would know everything, and it would be too much to know.

Sam understood that refusing to listen to secrets meant her friends thought she was cold and unfeeling. And that was exactly what she wasn't. But she acted that way because she longed to live as normal a life as possible for as long as possible. She loved having friends to walk with or go to coffee with in the morning when she took a break from writing.

But she couldn't let them count on her. When the gift appeared, which it would, she'd have to disappear from their lives. It was possible she could never see them again because of what she would know. Sam thought that if they understood why, they'd either forgive her or hate her.

So she could never tell. After all, how could anyone want to be friends with someone that could see everything you remembered? No one had clean, pure memories. Everyone was messed up in some way.

So she was elusive. Like a butterfly, people said. A black monarch, perhaps. They'd ask, "Who are your parents? Where are they? Can we meet them?" *Oh, God,* she would say to herself. So instead she told them as little as possible. She didn't know her father. Just that he had green eyes and dark hair like her. That's all she had ever been told. And her mom was a hermit living off in the mountains by herself. An artist.

They knew her mother's name when she told them. "Serenity Rivers is your mother? Her art is fantastic," they would shriek. "Aren't you proud to be her daughter? She paints like you write," one of her friends said one day.

That was something she had never thought about before. But it made sense. They both used their art to rid themselves of memories. Her grandmother did the same by planting gardens. A riot of color, if she remembered correctly. And then Sam laughed to herself. If she remembered correctly. That was the joke about the Rivers women. Remember. That's all they did. If there was a way to take those memories and slam them behind a steel door and never open it again, she would gladly do it. Anything to be normal.

Please, she said to herself, *make that be possible.*

And that was why she was heading to her grandmother's house. Not just because her mother had called. Not just because her grandmother was sick. Something had to be done. She couldn't continue to live her life this way, and if there was a solution, then it might be found in that old house where Rivers women had always lived.

That meant she was going to swallow her pride and ask, "Please. Make it stop." And if it couldn't be stopped, what point was there in living? If she couldn't find out the answer there, there was no point in going on.

So far, the trip had been without incident. She had stopped at gas stations that looked deserted, slipped into the bathroom, and then went to the store to buy snacks and food for the road. Each stop was quiet, and Sam was grateful for the feeling of normalcy she had been granted.

A few hours from her hometown, she had to make a stop at a busy truck stop. Drinking soda while driving was never a good idea, but she had wanted her diet Dr. Pepper so badly she had broken down and gotten one. The price for that indulgence was a stop she would not normally make. Sam pulled the car into the lot as far away from everyone as possible. It would mean a long, uncomfortable walk to the restroom, but as always, trying to avoid people made life hard.

It happened just as she reached the restroom door, and if she hadn't needed to pee so badly, she would have turned and run. Instead, she saw something she didn't want to see. Not that it was a bad memory. This one was mostly good. An older man was hugging and kissing a boy on the forehead. She felt a mix of kindness and danger flooding over her.

Luckily, it didn't last long. She had managed to stop it from continuing, and she didn't even look around to see where the memory had come from. Later, when she saw a picture of the boy, it took a moment to remember where she had seen him before. And she realized that it was the feeling of danger that should have made her keep watching.

If she would have, perhaps what came next could have been avoided. But then, probably not. At least, that's what she told herself.

Five

The quiet village of Lazy Rivers was full of upset people, reminding Randy Carver of a beehive that had been disturbed. It even sounded like one as people gathered in clusters on front porches, coffee shops, diners, and street corners whispering together. The buzzing sound of conjectures, thoughts, and fears.

"It's like before," people whispered to each other.

What's like before? Before what? Randy asked himself. He didn't know what they were talking about, but he wanted to know. He wanted to be part of the excitement that seemed to be everywhere.

He had stopped at one of the two coffee shops in town on his way to the next job, where he was replacing a decrepit-looking porch with new composite decking. He loved his work. It was never the same, and there was always plenty of it. Plus, he learned things he would never have known otherwise. Who would have thought being a handyman would be so rewarding?

Well, his dad did. Handyman's work was what his dad had done his entire life and took his only son along with him on jobs from the time he was ten. By fifteen, Randy was even better at most of it than his dad, which had made his dad proud and his mother happy, knowing he would always have something to turn to.

When he first came to Lazy Rivers, he always worked alone, but over time he had met the other handymen in town, and they often called each other in for jobs. Although working with a crew went faster, and he enjoyed their company, he also loved the jobs where he worked alone. It gave him time to think while being productive.

Lately, he'd been thinking about moving on. Which sounded crazy since he'd only been in Lazy Rivers for a short time, but he already had a good thing going, and he'd have to start again if he moved. But unlike his dad, he didn't seem to find comfort in settling down. He needed something more. What, he didn't know.

But unless something changed, he was thinking he'd pack up and move himself to a new town soon. For now, though, the town buzzing like a beehive had gotten him curious, so he asked the woman making him his fancy coffee drink what was happening. She shrugged and said some boy was missing, as if she were talking about a stray cat.

"What boy?" he asked, trying to keep the disdain for someone who didn't care out of his voice.

She shrugged again. Randy paid for his drink and stepped out of the store onto the wide sidewalk that held pots of flowers that he knew the garden committee maintained. It was a pleasant town. In some ways, he'd hate to leave it. And now there was the mystery of a kid missing. Not that he wanted a kid to go missing, but at least it might keep him in town longer.

He could hear his mother telling him that his boredom about normal things and his love of mysteries would get him into trouble one day. He'd laugh and say that it would be good trouble, not bad. She'd chuck him on the back of the head as they both laughed. Sometimes she'd add, "Seriously, Randy, be careful," like she knew something he didn't. His mother had been a mysterious woman herself. She always seemed to know what was happening before anyone else did.

But she kept it to herself most of the time. She'd say that nobody liked a busybody, and when she told people something she knew, that's how it came across. Even his dad wasn't all that interested in hearing what his mother said, and wanting his dad's approval, Randy followed his lead.

So when his mother died in her sleep from what was later determined to be an aneurism, he wondered if she had known and simply not said. And he was bereft. Not only because at eighteen he lost his mother, but also his wisdom guide. He didn't know how much she had silently guided him until she wasn't there anymore.

Everything was different after that. His dad stopped caring about almost everything except sitting in front of the TV with a beer and a bowl of snacks. His parents had been frugal, so the life insurance money and their savings were plenty for his dad to live on. The days of working together were over.

That was when Randy made his first move. He left town because he was bored. That's what he told himself, but it was really because no one needed him there anymore. And he couldn't stand working alone in places he and his dad had worked together. Which meant he had to choose a new place to be. He would learn something new, see new sights, and then move on.

Lazy Rivers was the fourth town he'd been in since he left home a year after his mother died. Now thirty, he doubted he'd ever settle down, but looking at the tree-lined streets of the town, he thought that if he did, it might be here, at least until he uncovered why it felt like a mystery lived here. He still called his dad every Saturday afternoon.

They'd have a brief conversation about the latest sports event, and he'd tell his dad he loved him and make him promise he'd call if he needed him, both of them knowing that he wouldn't. Need him or call him if he did. Which is why Randy had recruited the next-door neighbors, who had lived there as long as his dad, to call him if anything went wrong. He sent them little gifts once in a while to thank them.

Whistling, Randy adjusted his baseball hat and strolled to his truck, hoping to hear more about what everyone seemed to be talking about or find someone to ask about it. If nothing else, maybe the woman whose deck he was fixing would know more.

He noticed a car he hadn't seen before as he was leaving town, which caused him to turn to look at the driver. Was it a stranger in town? He had a brief glimpse of a woman with long, dark hair. He didn't think he knew her. To Randy, that meant there was someone new to meet. Looking in his rear-view mirror, he caught her looking back at him in hers. Dark green eyes. Beautiful. Another mystery to solve. Yet, another reason it might not be time to move on yet.

Six

For Sam, seeing the man's dark brown eyes in her rear-view mirror was a warning. Not that men didn't always look at her. Beauty was something she had, didn't necessarily want, but like all Rivers women, she was stuck with it and understood that it could be a gift or a burden. Both of which the Rivers women had all learned to deal with. The only thing they couldn't use it as was a weapon.

Sadly, Sam had met both men and women who did exactly that. Their memories scared the crap out of her, so she stayed away from them as much as possible. So she was used to men and women looking at her. But something about the man's eyes told her he wouldn't just look at her; he'd want to know her. That made him dangerous.

Why in the world had she looked back at him? Passing his truck, she had a glimpse of a tall, thin man with unruly brown hair and she gave into curiosity. Never a good idea. Now she felt like running and going somewhere else other than her grandmother's house. She was good at leaving, not staying. Between the man, the town, her grandmother, and her mother, there was going to be trouble for her.

Besides, she felt uneasy in Lazy Rivers. For as long as she could remember, it felt like something was wrong. Not just in her family, but in town. And she hated that the town had their same last name. Rivers. Lazy Rivers. What a stupid name.

People constantly asked her, "Did you Rivers women bring the river here or did the river bring the Rivers women?" Especially when they called her Lazy Rivers. It wasn't curiosity or teasing. It was bullying. Samantha knew it was because they were afraid of her and her mother and grandmother and all the Rivers women who had come before her.

Some people in town called them witches. Which they weren't. They practiced no craft. They were just like everyone else. Except for the one thing they could do and what she hated being able to do. See memories. *Why, in God's name, could they see memories? What use was it?* She had spent many nights crying herself to sleep over what felt like such an injustice. She yearned to be normal. Know things, or not, the way everyone else did.

As far as she knew, every Rivers woman had the gift, so why would she get a pass? She remembered what it was like to live without the gift. For the first ten years of all their lives, they were blissfully normal. Then one day, soon after their tenth birthday, they'd see something that had happened before. Even if they had been warned, nothing could prepare someone for that first time.

Sam remembered her first memory, the one that wasn't hers. It came from a boy in school. Until that moment, she had liked him. A lot. He was cute, funny, and very popular. One day, he turned around in class and said something to her. She never heard what he said. It was probably something trivial. But the memory wasn't.

She saw him hit his little sister with a plastic bat. Hard. When his mother came into the room to find out why she was crying, he said she had fallen. His sister didn't contradict him. She said, "Yes, that was what happened." The classroom had faded away during that moment, and she was so disoriented when it was over that the teacher had asked if she was okay. Like the little girl in the memory, she said that she was.

But she wasn't. Of course, she knew about the gift. Her mother had told her all about it. But both of them had hoped she hadn't received it, that she would go through her life never having someone else's memory play like a movie in her head. Not entirely like a movie though, because feelings came with it. All of them. The good, the sad, the ugly, the mean, the compassionate, the happy. All of them. It was hard enough to have your own feelings and then to have someone else's all at once. It wasn't a good gift to have. At all.

Thankfully, her first memory didn't carry all the feelings; otherwise, Samantha didn't think she would have been able to continue that day. Maybe that's why it didn't include the feelings. The gift was easing her into it. Her first reaction to the memory was disgust, then anger, and then the desire to tell him she knew what he had done. But both her mother and her grandmother had warned her to never do that. Don't blurt out what you see.

So she kept quiet. But from that moment on, she stayed as far away as possible from the boy, and every time she saw his sister, she tried to give her extra attention. That girl eventually ran away from home when she was a teenager and was never seen again. Or at least that was the story. Sam had always wondered if that was what had happened.

That boy's memories might have been the first she had seen of abuse, but it wasn't the last. And each one burned a hole in her heart because she had no power to stop it. They were over and done with. Not the future. The past. It took many lovely memories to keep just one bad memory out of her dreams. And sometimes there weren't enough of them to go around.

For a few months as a teenager, she had tried using her gift as a weapon even though she had been warned that it would backfire. And it did. She'd scare people with what she knew. She thought that meant they would leave her alone. Instead, it got worse. Eventually, she did what she had been told to do. Keep it to herself. But sometimes she felt as if she would explode.

After passing the man in the pickup truck, she was afraid. Not just because of him, but because as she drove down Main Street, she felt the buzz of the town, and that scared her. There was no way she wanted to be part of what was going on. So instead of driving through town north to her grandmother's house, she took a left and headed out of town. She wasn't ready for this. She'd go to the closest town instead and think things through. Spring Falls wasn't too far away, just far away enough to decide what to do next.

And although she had visited the town once with her mother, just to see where Lazy Rivers turned into the falls they named the town after, she knew no one would recognize her. Perhaps she would change her name while she was there. She'd done it before. People in Spring Falls would probably know the Rivers' name.

She'd be Samantha Warren—the pretend last name of the father she never knew.

Seven

To Serenity's surprise, when she returned home, her mother was not in the bedroom but sitting in the one comfortable chair in the living room. She had gotten it for her a few years ago and had it sent to her from the store. She had made sure that the men bringing it would show her how to pull the lever, so it made an extension for her legs.

Lizzy smiled at her daughter, and Serenity tried to smile back instead of scolding her for being out of bed. But she couldn't help herself. Seeing how tiny and frail her mother looked in the chair, she said, "What are you doing up?"

"Not ready to die yet," was her answer.

As if you had a choice, Serenity thought, while knowing that she probably did, given her mother's stubbornness. Well, all their stubbornness. Perhaps they had to be in order to survive so many memories that weren't theirs.

"Well, if you are going to be there, let me at least make you comfortable."

A few minutes later, she had a pillow under her mother's knees and a light blanket over her against the chill of the house.

"Hungry?"

She didn't wait for the answer. She knew Lizzy would probably say no. Instead, she made a pot of coffee and a few slices of toast. She brought a tray for her mother, propped it on her lap, and then pulled a chair up closer to her so they could eat together.

"Maybe you need this chair more than me," Elizabeth said, watching her daughter grimace as she lowered herself into her chair.

Serenity shook her head. "We all need a little work here," she said as she waved her hand to include the two of them and the house.

"Agreed," her mother sighed as she laid her head back in the chair. "Start right away, will you? Maybe start with your studio so you can keep on working."

Serenity didn't let the shock of her mother so readily agreeing to fixing the house show, but inwardly wondered what it meant. Getting her to do anything that wasn't her idea had always been a trial.

Instead, she smiled and said, "What about all of it at once? Do you know anyone who could handle it? Not just the house, but the yard and drive."

"It will be expensive, won't it? But I have money," Elizabeth said. "What I don't have is any idea who to hire."

Both of them knew that was because Lizzy had been a recluse most of her adult life. Staying in the house by herself. Doing god knows what, Serenity thought. But then, had she been much better than that herself? Serenity wanted to ask her mother how she had money, but didn't bother. Eventually, Lizzy would have to share all the information needed to continue running the house with her. This was just the beginning.

It seemed pathetic to her that she knew nothing at all about her mother's life. Even when she was still living at home, she hadn't known. But then, not sharing was the Rivers' tradition. After all, she'd done the same thing with her daughter. As her mother drifted off to sleep, Serenity removed the tray, shuffled into the kitchen, washed the dishes, promised herself to have a dishwasher installed, and called her daughter again.

Maybe she could get her to come home now, and the three of them could live together and learn from each other while there was still time.

Twenty miles away, Sam saw that her mother was calling and decided not to answer. But she was worried. Maybe her mother knew that she had returned. However, when she listened to the message, she was relieved. Serenity was asking her when she thought she'd be there.

But it was only a momentary release. Eventually, she'd have to go home, and what would they both say if they learned she had been so close and still didn't have the guts to go home? *It is what it is,* she mumbled to herself as she drove into Spring Falls. First she'd have to find a place to stay, and then she needed food. Perhaps check out the campus. She remembered it being a pretty place to walk. And see the falls, of course. There was a book brewing in the back of her head, and that might help her see more of what it was going to be. She'd go to Lazy Rivers. Just not right away.

Serenity smiled to herself as she left the message. She didn't know where Sam lived now; she was always moving. But she was sure that Sam would return soon to Lazy Rivers, and when she did, she'd help restore the house and maybe decide to stay. But first Serenity needed a nap, and then she'd deal with what needed to be done with the house.

All the bedrooms except her mother's were upstairs. She remembered when she would take the stairs two at a time. Now she grunted at every step. And she'd have to make it back down again. She wasn't sure who was making the most noise—her with her whizzing and grunting or the stairs as they squeaked and groaned. Her bedroom was at the end of the hall, but she wanted to turn it into her studio. It had the most light and the best view. Or maybe the room below it. It had the same light, and she could walk out into the garden. Well, what was once a garden, and she'd make it into one again.

Serenity was well aware that it was the light and view from her bedroom window had inspired her to paint when she was a girl. She didn't paint scenes. She painted light with all its colors and waves and dancing. Standing in the room now, even with the musky smell and the old paint peeling off the walls and ceiling, she loved this room because of those memories.

In her mind's eye, she saw the future of the room. The entire house, really. After a fire destroyed the first house on this land, the builders constructed this one to last. It had good bones, that's what people would say. Land was another thing she needed to find out about. How much land did they own? She had heard as a girl that their land extended well past the river that she could see from the window. The river had also inspired her painting.

She supposed it was called the Lazy River because it meandered through the countryside, taking its time. She knew people used to tease her mother when she was young. Instead of Lizzy Rivers, she was called Lazy Rivers, and she had even heard people call her daughter that. Somehow, she had escaped that torture.

Serenity shook her head. She never understood why people had to be so cruel. She believed in the innate kindness of people, but people often tested that belief. Especially when she saw some of their memories.

Although the bed was old and creaky, she had brought sheets and blankets with her, knowing her mother would still be using the ones they had when she was a child. So when she stretched out on the bed, she was grateful that for a moment she could pretend she was back home. Her home in the mountains. Not this ancestral home.

She let herself believe that illusion as she drifted off to sleep, knowing when she woke up she'd be back in the old creaky house. And worst of all, she'd have to go into town and ask around for people who could help her with the work that needed to be done.

Downstairs, Elizabeth heard Serenity's old bed creak and smiled to herself. Having Serenity home was going to be the best thing that ever happened to her. And then when Sam got there, it would be like heaven.

But first, they had things to fix. And not just the house. It was much more than that. It's why she couldn't die yet. She couldn't leave things as they were.

<h1 style="text-align:center">Eight</h1>

The next morning, Serenity had another surprise. Her mother was wide awake, sitting in her chair, and reading a book. Her mother was reading a book! Where did the book come from? What book?

Lizzy looked up and answered that question by saying, "Look at what book I'm reading," turning it around so Serenity could see. It was one of Sam's books. Serenity wasn't sure which one it was because she had read none of them.

And now her mother had. Had the world turned upside down?

"Did you like this one?" her mother asked innocently, but Serenity felt the jab behind it. Her mother had guessed she hadn't read it.

She could lie and say she had, but chose instead to admit that she didn't read her daughter's books.

"You're afraid, aren't you? But of what?" Lizzy asked. "That she will reveal something or share something that will trigger you? Or embarrass you? Or make you feel guilty?"

Serenity sat down in the nearest chair and said, "All of those reasons, I suppose."

Lizzy held out her hand, and reluctantly, Serenity took it. She had never enjoyed touching, and now her mother's hand was old, no longer the one she remembered as a child. But then her hand was old too. *Time flies,* she thought with regret and anger.

That was the thing. She was angry. But at what or who, she wasn't sure. Life maybe. This stupid gift. At least when you get a proper gift and you don't like it, you can give it away, take it back, or exchange it. Not this one. They were stuck with it, for better or worse.

Like a marriage, she thought, except none of them ever married. For a fleeting moment, she let herself think of Lucas. His green eyes and dark hair. Not tall, really, but definitely handsome. Here today, gone tomorrow like all the River's men.

"There's nothing in these books to worry about. Sam may have seen memories that served as inspiration for some stories, but all writers draw inspiration from everything around them, including their memories and things they have observed. Or curious about. Or where ever their muse takes them. Like your paintings. Just different. You use colors, brush strokes, and space on a canvas, and she uses words on a page."

Serenity hung her head. She knew her mother was right. But she wasn't ready. The books that Sam always sent her when they were published were packed and on their way. Perhaps when they arrived, she'd start one. Or not.

"And your gardening, mom. You do the same thing with the garden, don't you?"

"Did."

"Well, maybe get well, and we can get you back out there," Serenity said as she leaned over and kissed her on the head. "I'm heading to town to try to scare up someone to help with the house."

"And deal with the stares, too, right?"

"And that," Serenity agreed.

Before leaving, Serenity took a quick walk, just to say she did. She made a quick breakfast of coffee and a piece of toast for both her and her mother and prepared to let herself be seen. She could pretend that no one would know her in town, but that was useless. She wouldn't be surprised to find out that the one car that had passed her on her walk yesterday had noticed her and sped directly into town and spread the word, "Serenity Rivers has returned."

She doubted it would be that benign. More likely it would be something like, "One of those freaky Rivers women is back." And then people would laugh and start telling stories. *You're exaggerating,* Serenity said to herself. *And even if you aren't, let's get it over with.*

Lazy Rivers embodied the definition of a small town in every way. There were only a few stop lights, two places to eat, two coffee shops, one grocery store, and a farmer's market every Saturday in the town square during the summer. And, of course, there is standard everyone-knows-everyone kind of gossip.

But the one thing that made it different from many small towns was that it had always been pretty. And Serenity knew that was something special. She had traveled to many places and there were not that many places where the people cared about the beauty of their town. This town did.

Now that she was returning, she wondered why. *Why did they care?* And because she was a businesswoman at heart, *where did the money come from?*

Although the center of town was only a few miles from home, there wasn't much to see on the way. Trees lined the road, and sometimes there were entrances you could barely see with long driveways like theirs that led to houses set back into the woods.

Once in a while there was a field and a farmhouse. All of which Serenity appreciated. No strip malls. *A good name for them,* she thought. *They were set in a strip, and they stripped away the beauty of the land.* She knew they had built a mall just outside of town in the other direction. Hopefully that would satisfy everyone's shopping urges, and perhaps it wasn't ugly.

Just before she got to town, Serenity passed a sign saying *Tate's Nursery.* She had forgotten about that place. Checking the rear-view mirror to see if anyone was behind her, she made a U-turn and headed back.

Pulling into the parking lot, a flood of memories came over her. Not someone else's, hers. She had loved this place. Lizzy would bring her, and they would stroll the aisles in the store and out into the nursery, imagining where each plant would go in their garden.

Stepping out of her car, Serenity took a deep breath and let the mix of smells drifting in the breeze wash over her. She felt the joy she used to feel here when she was young, before the gift happened. For a moment, she forgot she was in potentially dangerous territory until she heard a man call out, "Serenity Rivers! I heard you were in town."

Instinctively, she shut down her feelings and turned to face the man. At first she didn't recognize him, and then she glimpsed the boy who had been her friend in school.

"Tom Tate, is that you?" Serenity said, surprising herself that she said that out loud.

Tom stopped a few feet from Serenity and let her look him over. He knew what she was doing. Trying to decide if she would let him get closer. In school, he saw her do it every day. Some kids laughed at her, but his mom had explained why she did it, and instead of laughing, he had yearned to be her friend.

And he had been for a while. Then she left town as soon as school was over, and he hadn't seen her since.

So he stood still and waited, knowing this time she would have to look. And maybe let him back into her life.

Appreciating Tom's stillness and being wise enough to notice the respect he was paying her, Serenity let herself remember the shy, skinny boy with reddish hair and freckles. The man in front of her still had some of that red hair, and his deep tan from working outside covered any freckles he might have had. But what hadn't changed was how she felt about him.

"You never laughed," she said, and she stepped forward to give him a rare hug.

<h1 style="text-align:center">Nine</h1>

Mama Tate stood inside the door of the nursery and watched the woman step out of the car and smiled to herself. Lizzy's daughter. All grown up. Still beautiful. Still nervous about being with people. But she was here, and that was enough for now. She watched as her son called out Serenity's name and then paused to let Serenity remember that he was a safe person. She was prouder than she could ever say of her son. He had always been kind and gentle, but he had grown wise and even strong over the years.

Even though she would like to take credit for the human that was her son, she couldn't really. She had only guided him. He was the one who had looked at the world that didn't like him because he was different and decided to be bravely different. With his husband, Brad, they had weathered the storm of disapproval and waited it out. For the most part they were accepted, and she was ready to turn the nursery over to the two of them.

So she watched with pride and joy as Tom paused and then smiled with happiness as Serenity reached out and hugged him, a rare gift from her. As she did, Tom's husband, Brad, stepped out from the gardens to say hello.

And he too stood still, not pushing anything, as Tom introduced him to Serenity. Mama watched as Serenity took Brad in. She thought that the Rivers women were like dogs. What they did was a form of smell. Taking in the essence of the person they were meeting. If you rushed them, they were forever leery. But wait and let them taste a memory or two, and if you passed the test, it wasn't as if you were instant friends, but at least you had a chance.

Long ago, Lizzy Rivers had let Ruth—but no one called her that anymore; she was Mama to everyone now—into her small inner circle of people she trusted. And the garden center had become a safe meeting place. It was as if the plants put a ring of protection around people when they were on the grounds.

Plants could feel people too, and Mama had often seen a plant turn away from people they didn't like. And that was one reason she was happy that Serenity had returned home. Only once in all the years she had been part of the nursery had she seen plants react to someone the way she had the day that man had walked through the aisles. For years she wondered if he was responsible for all those missing boys. Mama didn't know for sure, but the Rivers women might be able to help find out.

Mama's thoughts were interrupted when Serenity reached out and shook Brad's hand. And then the three of them walked towards her. She waited. Serenity didn't pause this time. Instead, without thinking, she stepped forward and hugged her, saying, "Mama!" And Mama Tate thought this was why she loved being called Mama. The sound of someone who didn't bestow trust lightly, calling her name with love, was her reason for existence.

As she hugged Serenity back, she felt her tremors and knew how hard it was for her to be here, to be hugged, to be trusting. Mama thanked the gods for first having been born in Lazy Rivers and for this nursery, where Mama met the young man whose father owned the Tate Nursery and then passed it on to his son.

Ted Tate had been—no, still was—the love of her life. They had many years together before he passed away. He too had seen that man that day and whispered to her, "Stay away from him." And she had. As much as she could. But looking back, she wasn't sure that had been the wise thing to do. Perhaps she could have stopped him. Now, this time, maybe she could, because this time she would have help.

"How's your mother?" Mama asked Serenity.

"Surprisingly well."

Mama chuckled, not mincing words, because what use was that? She said, "So she got sick enough to bring you home, but now she's getting better."

Serenity paused and thought about it before answering and decided that perhaps that was exactly what had happened.

Squinting at Mama, she asked, "Do you know why?"

"Other than wanting her daughter and hopefully her granddaughter to come home?"

Tom and Brad had stepped back from the two of them to give them space. But now they looked at each other and realized that there was more going on than just that Serenity had come home to visit. Mama hadn't told them anything was wrong, but she had seemed different lately. At first they asked her about it, but when she had shook her head and said, "Don't be silly," they had backed off.

Mama was a warm, loving friend to all living things kind of person, but at the same time, Tom had always thought she reminded him of a bull. She was kind of built like one too. With jeans, boots, and some kind of message t-shirt on she looked as if she could take anyone on. So most people never crossed her. And besides, she was almost always right, no matter what she was talking about. She didn't just think she was right; she was. She never cared if you agreed with her or not. That was your choice, but don't make her mad by doing something wrong intentionally.

On the other hand, Mama had a lightness about her that often showed up in her sense of humor. The t-shirt Mama was wearing today was an example. On the front it said, "Time flies like an arrow," and on the back it said, "Fruit flies like a banana." It had taken Tom a moment to get the joke about the banana. And he wasn't sure time flew like an arrow. To him, it seemed that it meandered, twisted around on itself, went backwards, jolted forward, slowed down, and sometimes stopped all together.

Watching his mother hug Serenity, he realized that to his mom the front of the t-shirt was a joke too. She knew how time worked. Except sometimes time did fly like an arrow. Too fast, straight to the grave. And that certainly wasn't funny. He missed his father, and if he could keep his mom and Brad with him forever, he would.

His mother's question to Serenity, "How can we help you today?" broke Tom out of his meandering thoughts.

Smiling at the three of them, Serenity said that she wanted to get the house and the gardens fixed up. Did they know anyone who could work on the house, and would they help with the garden?

"How bad is it?" Mama asked.

Serenity just shook her head.

"You know what? I think I'll just go visit with your mom right now. You stay and talk to Tom and Brad; pick out some plants with them, and they can tell you about that new handyman in town. He's cute enough. They would have noticed him."

Tom shook his head. No one could ever say his mother was afraid of saying what was on her mind.

Without breaking stride, Mama had her keys in her hand and was heading to her pickup truck. On the way, she grabbed a few pots of flowers and put them carefully behind the front seat.

"Just to get us started," she said as she spun out from the parking lot and headed back to Serenity's house.

The three of them stood and watched her go. Tom shook his head and said, "That's my mama."

All three of them knew that she wasn't just heading to see Lizzy and bring her a few pots of flowers. Something was going on, but they didn't know what it was.

Serenity said what they were thinking: "They'll let us know what's happening, won't they?"

"Eventually. Or you'll know yourself," Tom answered.

That's what Serenity was afraid of, and she realized that Tom understood that. She had forgotten that she had a friend in town after all. Something told her she was going to need all the friends she could get. Something was happening, and she wasn't going to be able to run away this time.

Maybe it was the reason her mother brought her here. Or one of the reasons. She knew there must be more. Whatever they were, she was going to be forced to do something she didn't want to do. That she was sure about. But she'd do it anyway.

Ten

Lizzy heard the truck coming up the road and knew who it was. She smiled and thought how lucky she was to have a friend like Mama. Mama would have figured out that she wasn't as sick as she said, and she would know why she had said she was. or even let herself become.

Not only would Mama not judge her harshly for that decision, she would applaud her. Mama believed that sometimes you needed to prime the pump to get things moving. And if pretending to be sicker than she said was what was needed to get Serenity and Samantha to come home, then so be it.

Besides, she really hadn't been feeling that well. She just wasn't dying. Not yet anyway. On the other hand, she might have pushed her luck and made herself sicker than she thought. Still, Serenity had done exactly what she knew she would. She would see Tate's Nursery on her way into town and pull in, and that would prompt the series of events that would bring Mama and her crazy t-shirts to her door.

Lizzy knew that Mama's son Tom had married a few years before. If there had been a big wedding, it hadn't been in Lazy Rivers,. It had probably been in New York, where his husband Brad had come from. Tom and Brad would have been worried about the fuss it would have made in town, and she couldn't blame them. She knew how judgmental people in Lazy Rivers could be, well, anywhere. People often didn't like what they didn't understand.

Still, Lizzy thought the town had become more open over the years, and she was counting on that to help bring her to do what needed to be done.

Mama knocked lightly on the door but didn't bother waiting for someone to open it. She never had. Why start now? Seeing Lizzy sitting in the chair, Mama sucked in her breath through her teeth and let it out slowly, hoping that Lizzy hadn't noticed. But of course she had.

"I'm not looking good, am I?"

"Nope."

"I'm happy to see you haven't lost your ability to tell the truth without hesitation or stopped wearing those crazy t-shirts."

Mama glanced down at her shirt and smiled before saying, "Did you do this to yourself, or is there something wrong?"

"Both." Lizzy answered. "But for now, let's assume I did this to myself so I can undo it, shall we?"

"Works for me," Mama said as she walked over to the chair and gently hugged Lizzy, feeling how thin she was beneath the worn-out t-shirt and sweats that she was wearing. *At least she isn't in her PJ's*, Mama thought.

Knowing what Mama was thinking, Lizzy said, "I changed, figuring you would be here."

"So you must also figure that we have something to discuss."

Lizzy looked at Mama and felt the worry that was sitting behind her eyes.

"It happened again?"

"It did. A boy is missing. Perhaps it's a coincidence, but you and I know that it's probably not."

Lizzy sighed. The decades-old mystery had been keeping her awake for months now. It was why she had broken down and done what needed to be done to bring Serenity home. Pretend to be dying, or at least she hoped that she was pretending.

Yes, she selfishly wanted Serenity home just for herself. But Lizzy knew that sooner or later she'd have to face what she had left undone, and she knew she couldn't do it without help. Facing it meant she would have to open herself to the town, the people, and their memories.

And she'd have to ask Serenity, and hopefully Samantha if she came home, to do the same thing. They wouldn't like it anymore than she did. Probably less, since they didn't have the stake in it that she did. They weren't carrying her guilt. She was the one who had shied away from facing the problem. But this time she knew she couldn't make that choice and live with herself, either here or the hereafter. The first time it happened, she had shut down. This time had to be different.

Something had to be done, and Lizzy knew it was Serenity who could do it. Because Serenity was different. Unlike her mother, who thought too much and did too little, Serenity took action. After all, she had taken the action of leaving town and then turning herself into a successful artist, and then taken action and come home.

Serenity wanted to change the world through her art, and perhaps she had. But now she'd have to help fix what was wrong right here in her own hometown.

If I could have done it myself, I would have, Lizzy thought to herself. But she knew she was just giving herself a pass for her lack of action in the past.

Mama watched Lizzy and felt her guilt and pain as if it were her own, because she knew Lizzy was blaming herself, but she was just as guilty of non-action as Lizzy was. Maybe more. But they were old now. Things needed to be completed. It was time to fix it.

"But before we start trying to fix the past and stop what is happening," Mama said, "Let's go into your garden and talk about its restoration."

As Mama helped her up, Lizzy thought that might be the theme of what was happening—restoration. Or was it redemption?

For the next hour, Lizzy and Mama let themselves disappear into the magical world of the garden. Of course Mama had to give Lizzy a hard time about how bad it looked and question her about how she could have let it get this way. Lizzy didn't mind. She knew the purpose behind it was to help her get up and get going. And that's exactly what she needed to do.

The June sun was warm as it rose in the sky, and finally Mama led Lizzy to the chairs that sat under the overhang formed by the second floor. The concrete patio was stained and dirty, and Mama made a mental note to have Brad come out and look at it. He was good at that kind of thing. Maybe he could handle the whole house.

"Thanks for coming to see me, Mama," Lizzy said, sipping the cold glass of water that Mama had gotten for her.

"Should have come before."

Both of them sat for a while, thinking about why Mama hadn't been back for so many years. There was a time when they saw each other almost every day. But one day, Lizzy saw one of Mama's memories. It wasn't a good one. And instead of keeping it to herself, she blurted out how sorry she was for what had happened.

Until that moment, they had both pretended that it didn't matter that Lizzy could see other people's memories. Not all the time, and it wasn't something she seemed to be able to control.

But Mama knew. Heck, everyone knew. It's why the town didn't care that Lizzy and her daughter stayed out of town. In fact, they almost demanded it. Now though the town was going to have to accept the Rivers women and their gift if they wanted to stop the person taking their children.

Both Lizzy and Mama thought they knew who it was. But were they right? Could they prove it? And could they stop him before it happened again? To do that, they'd have to start at the beginning, and that would mean using every skill they had.

Mama had tenacity, determination, and the good will of the town, which loved her and the beauty she helped bring to Lazy Rivers. Lizzy had the ability to see what had happened, or at least a version of what had happened, but to do that she would have to see into people. Nobody liked that, especially Lizzy.

"Shall we talk about the first time?" Mama asked.

Lizzy nodded, exhausted before they even began, because she knew that the first time that they knew about was probably not the first time at all.

How many children had there been? And had it only happened here in Lazy Rivers?

Eleven

"Are you heading into town?" Tom asked. "Since Mama went to see your mother, maybe we could catch up over food?"

Brad smiled at the two of them and said, "Go for it. I've got this."

Serenity hesitated as she always did, the habit of keeping people at arms length kicking in. But she knew what Tom was doing. He was choosing to buffer the reaction to her being in town, and she was grateful. Of course they might all be also whispering about the fact that she was with Tom, but at least they wouldn't just be staring at her. Besides, she needed help, and Tom knew everyone. He had stayed in town and faced the whispers and hatred, and she had run away.

"Yes," she answered.

"Your car is probably cleaner than my truck," Tom said.

Turning to Brad, he hugged him and softly said, "Thank you," trying not to let tears come to his eyes as he did. He didn't know how he had deserved someone as kind and understanding as Brad but he was grateful every minute of the day for him.

Neither of them said anything as Serenity drove the last few minutes into town, both because there was too much to talk about and getting started now wasn't a good idea, and Serenity was taking in the town she thought she knew so much about.

"It's changed," she said to herself out loud.

"It's been a while since you've been here," Tom answered. "We have more than one place to eat and two coffee houses instead of one! We even have two stop lights now."

Serenity laughed. "Such a big town!"

Tom pointed to a parking space in front of the old diner. "Might as well return to the scene of the crime."

Serenity knew what he meant. The old diner with it's blue and white awning protecting the front door from rain and snow was where the outcasts would escape to after school. And sometimes during school to either celebrate or escape the mind-numbness of classrooms taught by teachers who wished they were someplace else.

It was where they would pretend for a moment that they were mischief-makers. They would do things like turn the salt shakers upside down or switch the salt for the sugar. Big crimes. But the other reason for going straight to the diner this time was because it was where all the "old-timers" would be. Both of them knew that they might as well get the stares over with, and once that was done, listen to the town news from the town gossips.

"That's new," Serenity said, pointing at the parking meters.

"Ah. Yes. Not sure why we have them. Supposedly the money goes to keeping up the roads."

The two of them stood on the sidewalk in front of the diner before going in. Serenity held her breath as Tom took a deep breath in and let it out slowly. They stood there partly to let the people stare at them now and partly because Tom knew Serenity had to do that even as a kid. She always had to prepare herself.

When he was a boy, Mama had told him why. Serenity was shutting down, the best that she could, the part of her that saw memories of people when she was around them. Not all the time. Not all the memories. And not always important ones. Sometimes simple things like seeing someone eating dinner or singing at church.

At the time, he had thought that would be such a wonderful thing to be able to do, but his mama had explained how it wasn't. She assured him when he got older he wouldn't want someone seeing what he had been up to at random times.

The Rivers women didn't like being able to do it, and neither did the people in town like that they could. There was always the question of what the Rivers women would see that would either embarrass them or put them in danger. That question worked both ways.

Now that he was older, Tom understood what his mother had meant. But he knew Serenity, and if she saw something he wished she didn't see, she wouldn't hold it against him. Without thinking, Serenity took Tom's hand as they made their way to a booth. In fact, she didn't even notice until they were seated.

"Sorry about that."

"I liked it." Tom said and meant it. He was honored. And worried. Did Serenity already know something that he didn't and was afraid of? It occurred to him that it might be that that was scaring her. One didn't need to see memories to know how upset everyone in town was. Again.

"The menu is the same," Serenity said, trying not to touch the menu that she thought might not have been cleaned since the last time she had been there. How long now? Twenty years?

"And so is the waitress," a voice said behind her. Serenity turned and saw a short, plump woman with curly gray hair pulled back into a bun and a pencil tucked in her ear, smiling at her.

"Betty Jean?"

Without thinking, Serenity stood and hugged her, forgetting for a moment to be worried. Betty Jean had been the waitress there for as long as she could remember. She was probably her mother's age. Maybe older, maybe younger. And she had always been kind to the two strange kids.

"I heard you were back in town. And you brought your friend with you," she said, smiling at Tom.

For a moment, Serenity stopped smiling, remembering why she was in town, but Betty Jean didn't let that last.

"Honey. Your mom is not as sick as she is pretending to be," she whispered. To answer Serenity's puzzled look, she added, "I know many things."

Out loud Betty Jean said, "Shall I bring your favorite meal?"

When they both nodded yes, Betty Jean turned to all the people in the diner and, with her hands on her hips, said. "Yes, Serenity is home. Now get back to your food."

Within seconds everyone turned away, Serenity's face turned pink, and then she started smiling. She had been worried about sneaking into town. It was better this way. Everyone had turned away and went back to eating, except the man sitting in the back of the room. Alex Williams, police chief, just kept on looking their way, not trying to hide that he was watching.

Was he claiming his right to be in charge, was he just being curious, or was there something wrong?

Twelve

One other person didn't turn away after Betty Jean scolded the room, but then Serenity didn't expect him to. It was his restaurant, after all. Betty Jean nodded at Joseph and headed to the kitchen to put in Tom and Serenity's order. She was happier to see them than they would ever know. She turned to look back at them as she placed their order and slowly let out the breath she didn't know she had been holding. She had been so worried, not sure what to do. But now, with Serenity home, things might get better. Or worse. Depending on how you looked at it.

Joseph stood in the doorway to the back room and didn't move, even when Betty Jean nodded his way. He wasn't about to be told what to do by anyone, not even Betty Jean, the waitress that kept his diner running. As his gaze swept the room, he caught Alex's eye. They stared at each other, acknowledging each other's authority. They knew each other well enough for Joseph to be sure that Alex was more than curious. He was probably as worried as he was. But probably not for the same reason.

Serenity Rivers in town meant trouble, no matter how you looked at it. Her mother had always been trouble, but Lizzy hadn't come to town in years, so it had stopped mattering. But now, here was her daughter, back in town after twenty years. That wasn't good. And, of course, she was with Mama Tate's boy, Tom. That wasn't good either. Tom had his own gift of observation. The two of them together again could be even more disruptive.

As he watched them, Joseph wondered if they were planning to switch the salt for the sugar, and despite his worry, he chuckled under his breath. Of course he had known they were doing that when they were kids.

Tom, feeling Joseph's eyes on him, nodded, acknowledging his presence. He felt his blood freeze for a moment when Joseph winked back at him. What did that mean? Tom knew Joseph had never been an expressive man, so every gesture counted. But even as taciturn as he was, at over six feet tall and almost half as wide, he filled the doorway the same way he filled the town's life.

Tom and Serenity had known, or known about, both Alex and Joseph their entire lives. The two men had a few things in common. First, everyone in town knew them and respected them for better or worse. And second, everyone did their best to stay out of their way, or if they couldn't do that, kowtowed to them. *Well, almost everyone,* Tom thought, thinking of Betty Jean.

He had chosen to try and stay out of their way. Of course, he had tried to stay out of everyone's way. He tried not to bring more attention to himself than necessary. But like Serenity, he had always been marked as different, and that had not been a good thing, at least to most people in town. Neither Serenity nor Tom had been friends with Alex. He was five years older than the two of them, so they rarely had direct contact. They only heard about him because, even as a kid, Alex had watched over, or ruled over, depending on your point of view, everyone he knew.

Being a police chief was the perfect job for Alex Williams. It gave him the right to know what you were up to. Depending on how you felt about being watched over, this was either good news or bad news. Joseph was much the same way, but he ruled from his diner and didn't seem to care for the people of Lazy Rivers.

Tom thought that perhaps being the owner of the diner was not something Joseph had wanted to be, and he only did it because it had been preordained for him. His dad and his father before him had owned the diner. It had belonged to the Trapp family from the moment it was built. Maybe trapped was how Joseph felt. He knew Joseph made money not just from the diner but also from a side business of hustling the sauces he made. That business kept him out of town a great deal. But when he was in town, no one missed that he was there. Although rarely talkative, he made his point just by being present.

As a child, Tom had always been slightly afraid of both men. Although neither of them had given him any trouble, he just wasn't sure what they thought of him. But it wasn't just that. Maybe Serenity would know why they had scared him when he was young. Maybe they still did. Turning his back on Alex and Joseph, Tom looked across the table at Serenity, wondering what she felt about the two men who refused to stop looking at them.

Or maybe they were just looking at her. For that, Tom couldn't blame them. She, like all Rivers women, was beautiful. Besides, it was hard to hide her red hair and striking blue eyes. For a woman as private as Serenity, it was probably just another burden to bear. He understood how it felt to be noticed and judged just from appearances.

As she picked up her coffee cup, he saw her hand shaking. Maybe Alex and Joseph scared her, too. Or maybe it was just the feeling of being stared at. Or maybe she was worried about what she would see if their memories became visible to her. Serenity saw Tom's look, put the coffee down, and smiled at him. "I'm okay. Now tell me how you are doing, and then maybe more about the missing boy everyone seems to be talking about."

"Are you sure?" Tom asked.

Serenity knew he was asking if she was sure about wanting to get involved with the town's problems. He was right. She was afraid of doing it, but she also knew that she couldn't turn away this time.

"Maybe we should start with the first time." Twirling the salt shaker, tempted to turn it upside down just for fun, even though she could feel Joseph's eyes on her, daring her to do it.

Letting go of the salt shaker, she added. "If it was the first time."

Tom nodded. He thought Serenity was right. It probably wasn't.

Thirteen

Samantha typed the last sentence in the paragraph, sighed, and leaned back in her chair. For the last few hours she had disappeared from what people called the real world and lived in the one she saw in her imagination.

She had been tempted to write in the coffee house a few blocks from the motel but stayed in her room instead, still not sure that being seen was a good idea. Someone could recognize her. Not likely. But possible. And then it would get back to her grandmother and her mother, and then, well, then she'd have to own up to the fact she was afraid to go home.

It was so much easier living in the world of her writing. Being a writer was what kept her sane. She even liked doing the business of writing, even though now she didn't have to do most of it. She had hired a virtual assistant who took care of the marketing and administrative end of writing. All she had to do was write and then have weekly meetings with Jan, her assistant.

She felt as though Jan understood her because they had worked together for years. Even though Sam knew that Jan had other clients, she always felt as if she was the only one. It was quite a gift. Someday perhaps they could meet in person. However, that was unlikely. Sam didn't even know where Jan lived. She was as private as the Rivers women.

She could just stay in, but now that the writing was done for the day—she could always tell when it was time to stop— she was restless, bored, and hungry. She'd have to go out sooner or later; it might as well be now. So far the only people Sam had seen in town were the man who had checked her into the motel and the woman at the local supermarket when she had bought groceries, mostly drinks, to keep in her mini fridge.

Fiddling with the pen she kept by her computer in case she had a thought that needed to be written down quickly, Sam decided she had to get out of the room or she'd go crazy. She'd wear her hair up under her hat, and with sunglasses on, no one would even notice her. But could she pull that off if she went out for lunch? And was it necessary anyway? Yes, t was. She was starving, and she couldn't hide forever.

Besides, she was only planning to be in Spring Falls for a few days, and if Lizzy and Serenity found out she had been there, she could simply explain that she needed a couple of days to finish up the book she was writing. That was true. She had scheduled the current book to be released in a few months, and she was running out of time. That was entirely her fault. She had chosen the date. But then she hadn't known that the book would take a twist she had to follow, which had taken the past week to write.

But the not knowing of writing was something she loved. She'd start with a general idea in mind and then let the story be told to her. Sometimes she thought she was just someone who simply wrote down the story she saw in her head. A scribe. Maybe all writers felt that same way. As for ideas, she had too many to worry about ever running out of one. Other people's memories often sparked an idea for a book and for scenes in it. For that reason, and that reason only, Sam had learned to like her gift a tiny bit.

At the moment, though, she was starving, and nothing in her little fridge was going to satisfy her. Pulling her long hair up into a ponytail that stuck out through the back of her hat and grabbing her sunglasses, she decided it was time to go to the restaurant down the street. Since Spring Falls was a small college town, there were more choices of places to eat than in Lazy Rivers.

She hadn't been in Spring Falls in years and wondered how much it had changed. It would be fun to explore, and she thought she could pass for one of the students, a little too old for one, but maybe no one would notice. She had two things to worry about. Being noticed and noticing. If she could just have a pleasant stroll to the restaurant and a quiet meal, she'd be happy.

Checking herself in the mirror by the door, she decided she looked okay. Grabbing her cell phone and credit card, she stuck the motel key into her pocket and ventured out.

It was a beautiful June day, and Spring Falls was a lovely town. Pots of flowers and small trees lined the broad sidewalk. Since it was June, there weren't as many college students, which worried her a little, but at the same time it meant she didn't pass as many people, eliminating the chance to see something she didn't want to see.

Half way to the restaurant, ParaTi's, she passed an art gallery and wondered if her mother had thought about having her art placed there. She made a mental note to ask her. She knew her mom had someone, like Jan, who took care of all the business end of her art, but still, Spring Falls wasn't that far from Lazy Rivers, so perhaps once she got the courage to go home, they could come back here together.

As she passed the gallery, she glanced in and caught a glimpse of a young woman, dressed in purple and green with blue spiked hair, and smiled. If she wasn't so afraid of people, she thought she'd enjoy someone like that to talk to. As she turned away from the window, she accidentally bumped into a woman pushing a stroller.

"Excuse me," the woman said, smiled, and walked away.

Sam stood and watched her go by, frozen to the spot. This was why she hated her gift. What was she supposed to do with the memory that flashed by? A man screaming at the woman, the baby screaming in the background, things being thrown, and a door slamming.

Nothing. There was nothing she could do. And it was that nothing that constantly brought her pain. Sam almost turned and went back to the motel, but she was too hungry, and she just couldn't live her entire life hidden away. Besides, she rarely saw more than one memory a day. Maybe this was her quota. Or if not, perhaps the next one would be a good one.

One can always hope, Sam muttered to herself, glancing once again into the window of the gallery, thinking that anyone who could dress like the woman standing on the ladder stringing lights probably had only good ones.

But then, for a moment, Sam saw one of the woman's memories that was full of darkness and confusion. It passed quickly, but it was enough to remind Sam that nobody escaped bad times. But what comforted her was seeing the bright happiness on the woman's face. Yes, it was possible to live through those times and still be happy.

The woman turned, saw Sam looking into the gallery, and waved, and just like that, a flood of happiness took over, and Sam waved back.

Remember, Sam said to herself. *Life can be good.* It was something she'd have to remind herself of often in the coming days.

Fourteen

Randy stepped back and admired his work. The porch, which had looked as if it would blow over in the next big breeze, was now beautiful and functional. He had used composite wood so that the elderly owners would no longer have to paint it every spring. To make it even safer, he installed two hand rails so they could easily get down the shallow steps he had made.

He had suggested maybe a ramp instead of stairs, but they both were adamant that they wanted stairs, so his solution to the problem they weren't ready to admit was shallow, broad stairs. It cost a bit more in materials than they paid him for, but he couldn't have lived with himself if they fell down the stairs because they were too steep for them.

As the woman handed him his check for the work, she reached out and hugged him, saying their new porch was beautiful and a blessing. He wasn't sure which he liked best, the money or the hug.

If he could live on hugs, he'd probably choose that, but life wasn't like that, so he thanked her for the check and turned to go to his truck.

"Have you heard anything about the boy?" She called out to him.

Turning back, Randy said, "Not really. Did you know him?"

"Not the latest boy. But the ones from long ago, I knew one or two of them."

"Wait, how many boys go missing from this town?"

She paused before replying. "It's been going on for a while. The first boy was the police chief's brother. Ages ago. Actually, one of them returned years later. Had just run away from home. That's when people started thinking that they were wrong about the boys being taken. Maybe they all just ran away. Maybe that's all that has happened with this boy."

"Possibly," Randy replied. "Let's hope so."

Leaning over to give her a kiss on her cheek, he said to call him if she needed anything.

"I will, young man," she answered.

His next job was all lined up. One he could complete in a day or two, and since he had finished this one sooner than he thought, he decided to treat himself to a lunch in town at the diner. Maybe pick up some news about the missing boy. He hoped the old woman was correct—that the boy was just a runaway. A missing boy was, for whatever reason, terrible, and he knew the parents would be frantic, but at least there would be more hope of finding him than as if someone had taken him.

By the time Randy arrived at the diner, it was lunch, and there were hardly any spaces left in the cramped parking lot. He squeezed his truck between a tree and another truck, hoping he left enough room for them to get in easily. There was one open stool left at the counter. He slid in and said "hi" to Joseph, who looked like a fixture in the doorway to the back room. Joseph barely acknowledged him. Joseph wasn't known for his gregarious nature.

Randy nodded at Betty Jean when she raised a finger to let him know she'd be there in a minute and tilted his head at the police chief sitting at the back of the diner, a little astonished that he had just learned something about him. He didn't know Alex Williams well, but he thought it was always good to acknowledge the people in town who ran the town, and right here in this diner were quite a few of them.

Betty Jean poured him a cup of coffee as she passed by to a table. Efficient as always, she didn't need to ask him if he wanted it. She knew already. "Same?" she asked as she poured. He winked, and she smiled, letting him know she'd be back with his french fries and burger in a minute. He didn't even have to say, "Hold the pickles," she'd know.

Randy thought that was the advantage of staying someplace. People got to know you. On the other hand, that could be a disadvantage, depending on who you were and what you wanted out of life. Until he saw that girl in his rearview mirror, he was of the camp that it was best to move on once people thought they knew you, but now he wanted to know her, whoever she was.

Besides, the town was growing on him. There was plenty of work, and if he could collect a few hugs along the way, maybe that would be enough to keep him here. That and the woman. Glancing around the room, he hoped he'd see her. Then he might be able to figure out if it was just a flight of fancy or something more. He was ready for something more.

However, he could have it all wrong. After all, he only saw a brief glimpse of her, but he swore there was a jolt of some kind. And did that mean there was something between them already? Another look around the diner assured him that there was not a dark haired beauty with deep green eyes. But there was an older woman with the same kind of beauty sitting with a man he knew to be Tom Tate. Neither of them paid any attention to him. They were busy talking.

He didn't know who the woman was, but he knew Tom. They had met when Tom and his husband Brad were doing the landscaping for a house he was working on. He hadn't had a chance to thank him for how good the landscaping had been. Now was the perfect time to tell him. That way, he could also find out who the woman was.

Yes, curiosity was either a gift or a burden, depending on how you looked at the consequences. But being curious was something he was, and he liked it. Even when it got him in trouble. But as he started to go over to tell him, the woman and Tom were already halfway out the door. He'd have to call him later.

Betty Jean slid his lunch across to him and said, "It's good to have Elizabeth's daughter back in town."

Seeing his puzzled look, she added, "Guess you haven't met her yet. Lizzy lives out of town, and now that her daughter Serenity is back, I bet they are going to need your services to fix up their house."

Randy said thanks, asked for directions, and said he'd go stop in and meet her. For a moment, Betty Jean thought of warning Randy about stopping in at Lizzy River's home unannounced, but then decided against it. *Let him find out for himself, and besides, with Serenity home, things could be different.*

"Do you know anything about the missing boy?"

"If you want the skinny, talk to Pete over there," she said, nodding at a man sitting at the end of the bar. Just then, the man sitting beside Pete took money out of his pocket and slipped it across the bar, saying, "Thanks, Betty Jean. See you Monday."

"Might as well go over and talk to Pete now then," Betty Jean said as she picked up Randy's plate and moved it next to Pete. Seeing he didn't have any choice in the matter, Randy grabbed his coffee and changed seats.

"Pete, this here is Randy. He's a handyman, kind of new in town, but curious about the missing boy. Perhaps you can fill him in? Randy, Pete owns a farm outside of town, near Elizabeth River's place, by the way."

With that introduction, Betty Jean headed off to the next customer, feeling proud of herself for putting the two of them together. Pete could use a young friend to talk to, and Randy might stay in town if he got more interested in what was going on. Lazy Rivers needed more young people. Perhaps Serenity was coming home to stay. That could be the beginning of a new era for the town.

The old-timers like her were tired. They loved their town and did their best to keep it a pretty town, but eventually someone was going to have to take their place. Betty Jean shook her head. She and Joseph were tired, but she didn't think anyone would want to do what they were doing for the town. That was most likely over. The problem was, neither of them knew how to end it.

Fifteen

"Serenity and Tom went to town. Perhaps we should bring them here and talk this over with them," Mama said.

She had taken Lizzy out into the garden, where they had discussed what needed to be done to it, both of them avoiding for as long as possible the subject of the missing children. But it got hot, and they got hungry, so now they were back in the house. Mama had ransacked Lizzy's refrigerator and made them both a grilled cheese sandwich. She made a grocery shopping list while she was at it. If Serenity wasn't prepared to go to the grocery store yet, she'd go herself.

Hearing Mama opening and closing cupboard doors, Lizzy called out, "I order food and they bring it."

"Well, when was the last time you did that? There's no fresh food in your house."

Helping Lizzy to the kitchen table, Mama put the sandwich and a glass of water on the table, saying, "Eat up. We can't have you up and dying from starvation just yet."

Lizzy reached out and touched Mama's arm. "I've missed you."

Mama bent over so that their foreheads were touching. "I missed you too."

Both of them sighed, thinking about how much time they had lost, both of them wishing they could take it back.

After taking a bite of her sandwich, she answered, "Yes, perhaps we should do this together," referring to Mama's question from a few minutes before about their children. Mama's cell phone buzzed on the table. Seeing who was calling, she winked at Lizzy as she answered, "Hey." After a few moments of listening, she said, "We were just thinking that."

Hanging up, Mama said. "Well, that takes care of that. Tom says he and Serenity were talking about the missing boy and thought you and I could fill them in on the past."

Lizzy felt a deep weariness settle over her. What she wanted to do was go back to bed and pretend to be dying, or maybe she was dying, and she was pretending to be living. Either way, she was tired. It felt as if her bones melted into sticks of licorice, and all she wanted to do was curl up and let go. But she had promised herself to repair her relationship with Serenity and perhaps, in the process, find a way to help her live a happier life. Serenity and Sam didn't have to live out a tradition that had been decided for them.

Somewhere in the past, for some unknown reason, Rivers women had decided that men were good to have around, but only for a brief time. Maybe one of them had gotten their heart broken, seen a memory that destroyed trust, and decided to take control by not letting that happen ever again, to any Rivers woman.

Whatever the reason, that decision had been passed down as an expected tradition. She knew her mother, grandmother, great-grandmother, and the women before them had obeyed it as if it were a law. But it wasn't, and if she had anything to do with it, she would not let it dictate the future.

As a young woman in love, she would have broken that tradition herself. She would have kept Matthew by her side. She would have figured out a way to not see his memories unless he told them to her and lived out a life together. They would have raised Serenity as a family.

"I still miss him," Lizzy said, her purple eyes brimming with tears.

She didn't need to tell Mama who she meant. And she appreciated Mama didn't say, "I told you so.' She had used all her persuasive skills to convince her to not let Matthew go. To not push him away. But she just couldn't listen; she didn't hear the words of her best friend. Instead, it was her mother's voice and her grandmother's voice reminding her what she needed to do. Push Matthew Nelson away. He had done his job. It was time for him to go.

"Maybe we can find him," Mama said.

Lizzy shook her head, picking at the crumbs of the sandwich. She hadn't realized how hungry she had been. There was nothing left of it. Maybe she wasn't sick. Maybe she had just been starving herself. *In more ways than one,* she thought.

"He's probably been happily married for years and has a boatload of children."

"Or maybe not. But even if he is, which I doubt, don't you think he would want to know that he has a daughter and a granddaughter?"

Lizzy shook her head again. "No. Then he'd hate me for not telling him. No, it's best left alone. Besides. We're old. He's probably dead."

But even as she said that, Lizzy knew that part wasn't true. She would know if he had died. Yes, he was alive somewhere, but she had no right to disrupt his life now. The best that she could do was help Serenity and Sam not make the same mistake. Well, Serenity already did. But she was young enough to fix it. And hopefully, Sam still had a chance. If she would only take it.

Glancing out the window, she saw Serenity's car making its way up the rutted lane to the house. In the winter, it was almost impassible. It hadn't mattered before. In fact, it helped keep people at bay. But now that Serenity was home, they'd have to fix it. Perhaps Mama would know who to hire for the house and driveway.

If it shocked Tom to see the state Lizzy had let herself become, he was careful to hide it. For a moment, Lizzy had a brief flash of one of Tom's memories. It was a happy one, but very private, and it made her look away for a moment before reaching to pull him into a hug.

"It's good to see you, Tom," she said, smiling at him. And it was. Serenity and Tom had been friends for a long time, two people fighting against the tides of what people were supposed to be like.

"And you," Tom said, his eye sweeping around the living room at the disrepair. He hadn't been in the house since Serenity moved away a long time ago, and he doubted that Lizzy had done anything to keep the house running well, let alone looking good.

Lizzy caught the look that he had tried to hide and said, "Yes. I know. I let it go, but I want to get it fixed up again."

Immediately Tom's thoughts went to Brad, who would love to get his hands on an old house. "My husband could help," and then froze. He knew Lizzy had never treated him any differently, but did she know he was married? Would she disapprove?

He needed not to have worried. Lizzy smiled and said, "Send him over, and we'll talk," and Tom let out the breath he hadn't known he was holding.

Serenity and Tom took seats on the other side of the kitchen table across from their mothers. It was the same one they had sat at when they were kids playing monopoly on rainy Saturday mornings. Serenity had always loved this table. It was old but beautiful. It was a yellow oval Formica table with steel rimming and legs that met in the middle to make two circles before fanning out again. The two ends dropped down, but Serenity couldn't remember it ever being done.

The table was in pretty good shape, and with a little cleaning, would look brand new. Not so much for the chairs, but maybe they just needed to be stuffed and covered again. They matched the table. She wondered if Tom knew anyone who could restore them.

Serenity realized she was distracting herself from the matter at hand. Dragging herself away from designing things, something she loved as much as painting, she asked, "Mama, who exactly is missing this time, and what do you remember from the first time?"

Lizzy and Mama looked at each other. Lizzy nodded, and Mama cleared her throat before answering.

"It probably wasn't the first time."

Sixteen

Coffee in hand, Matthew Nelson opened his computer, ready to check on what was happening around the world. It was what he did every morning, and if he was truthful, which he tried to be, what he did a few times a day. Reading about the world was the best that he could do now. He had retired a few years before, and now he wasn't sure why he had done it. Was it because of the expectation to retire when one gets older?

Now, Matthew was wondering if he had agreed to a story about a lifestyle that he didn't want to live. Where was the adventure of life? Puttering around the house, going for walks, and trying and failing to write a book was not working.

It used to be him traveling around the world and writing about what he saw. He was the one who reported the good, the bad, and the ugly things that went on. His words were the ones people read.

He always wrote in a way that didn't sensationalize a story. He reported it and looked for solutions. It was exhausting.

But now, retired, he had to satisfy his curiosity about the world by subscribing to every online newspaper he could. He read articles written by people he had known for years. They were still working. Why wasn't he?

But he knew why. It wasn't only because he was old that he had retired. It was because he had come home to take care of his elderly parents, who died within days of each other. However, he got to spend a last year with them and was glad he had done so. But now he was still here with nothing to do. He had sold their home, and he had moved into an apartment, settled the estate, and he still hadn't moved on. He was wondering why. Probably because he didn't know what to do next.

So he read the online news. And then wrote what he thought about it. Just because he was retired didn't mean he could stop himself from writing. It was what he did. However, it felt useless now because it went out to no one. He knew he could post on social media but couldn't bring himself to do it. Maybe he just didn't understand how it worked well enough or because he hated most of the channels. Which was why he was trying to write a book. It wasn't going well.

Perhaps it was because he wasn't part of the action. He wasn't there. All he was doing was observing what others said, and who knew what to believe these days? His one guilty pleasure, guilty only because he should have given it up years before, was the weekly online newspaper, if you could call it that, from Spring Falls. Not because anything happened there, but because he had once, for a short time, called it home.

He hadn't grown up there but had ended up in the small community college. It was partly because it was inexpensive. His parents didn't have enough money to put him through school, and he had to pay for it himself. But there was another reason for going there. He had heard about a man who taught a writing class who had once been what Matthew dreamed of becoming. A journalist.

Spring Falls had been a blessing in so many ways. The teacher he had gone to study with became his mentor and later helped him get his first job. It was also when he had met the love of his life.

She hadn't been his first love. His first love had been a girl he had gone to high school with. Both of them knew they would not be together forever, but they had a summer filled with lovely times before college. And when they said goodbye, he had almost gone back and said he was wrong. They should stay together.

But he hadn't. Instead, he had done what he had promised himself he would do and went off to college. After a few letters and phone calls, they had drifted away from each other. At their last high school reunion, the first one he had attended because he hadn't been somewhere else in the world when it was being held, they hadn't even recognized each other.

She had laughed and said he was still quite handsome, but she hadn't known him now that his once-red hair was now gray. And he graciously said the same to her. But truthfully, he hadn't known her at all. He had to look at her name tag to know who she was.

But the love of his life? That was different. He thought he would know her anywhere. But would Elizabeth Rivers know him? He thought so. Maybe their looks had changed, but they knew each other differently from how they looked. Yes, Lizzy had been beautiful. Maybe she still was. But it was how he felt when he was with her he didn't think would ever change.

So even though he justified that he read the Spring Falls news online because he had once lived there, he knew it was also because he might also read something about the town, Lazy Rivers. It wasn't that far away from Spring Falls, so it was possible if something happened there, the Spring Falls News would report it.

Still, he knew it was stupid for him to keep reading it, hoping for who knew what. Lizzy Rivers had made it clear that she wanted nothing to do with him. She had pushed him away and made him promise to stay away. And even though he had searched his memory for something he might have done wrong, he never could figure out why it had happened. Still, she said if he really loved her, he would keep his promise and stay away.

And he had done just that, stayed away. But now would it matter? She might not be alive anyway. And that was what he was afraid of. He would see it online, and it would break his heart. But knowing Elizabeth, they still might not report it. She was the most private and stubborn person he had ever met.

Looking around his small apartment, Matthew realized what was wrong. He was bored out of his mind. He was used to traveling, writing, and seeing new places. Maybe it wasn't too late to do that again. Travel. Maybe write about it. Not for the newspaper, for himself. Maybe learn more about the best places to post writing. There were so many places to post writing these days. Especially since he didn't need to make money from it. He just needed to be doing something.

And if it just happened to take him through Spring Falls, so what? He would be visiting his alma mater. However, Matthew thought that there was something else he also wanted to do there. There was a mystery to solve. Maybe more than one, since he didn't know if they were connected. It was an old one, but perhaps he could research it and then write about it.

Heck, Matthew thought. Forget the traveling all over. *I'm going back to Spring Falls.* But he promised himself that he would not go to Lazy Rivers. He would not try to find out what happened to Elizabeth Rivers. He wouldn't. But even as he promised himself, he knew he would probably break that promise. He had to know.

Now he knew it was time to go. No one would miss him here. Well, maybe the barista at the coffeehouse he stopped in every morning, but that was it. There was no one left in his family. And the friends he made were all over the world. They didn't care where he lived.

He was too healthy to stop doing what he loved. He paid rent month to month, used to traveling and staying nowhere for long, so if he packed up now and left, it would be okay. Since he was a traveling journalist at heart, he always traveled light, and the last year had changed none of those habits.

Spring Falls was just a day's drive away. He could be there by nightfall.

Seventeen

"What do you mean, it probably wasn't the first time?" Serenity asked.

Mama and Lizzy looked at each other, and when Lizzy nodded at her, Mama said, "Well, the first boy we know about happened fifty years ago. In fact, it was when I was pregnant with you. But at the time, no one thought there was someone taking kids. Everyone just assumed he had run away. He didn't have the best family life. In fact, it was pretty terrible. He came from a family that just kept having kids. We all knew the dad was mean. And of course the mom was so exhausted she couldn't do anything about it, and then she died, which made it worse.

"Zack just didn't fit in. He was small for his age, quiet, withdrawn really, not a farmer, which is what he was expected to be. So he was either ignored or pushed around. Probably worse than that. Because of his family life, we all thought he had just left.

His father thought that too. He did little more than shrug when he realized he was gone. Although he may have never said, 'It's just one less mouth to feed,' it was obvious that's what he felt."

"How old was he? Has anyone tried to find him since then?" Serenity asked.

"He was ten, And I don't think so. Maybe the kids that were left with their parents were angry that they had been left behind, so they didn't care to look for him when they grew up. Who knows? Over the years, the kids slowly left town. Finally, the dad died. Just as bitter and mean as always.

"Only one son stayed in town, the youngest. He was five when Zach left, or was taken, so Alex probably doesn't remember him at all. But he didn't want to be a farmer, either. As soon as his dad died, he sold the farm to the farmer who lived next to them. By then it was a wreck, so I heard he didn't get much for it, but at least he got away from that mess. About ten years ago, he was elected to be the police chief."

"Alex Williams?" Serenity asked, surprised that they had just seen him at the diner. She saw him the minute they came in the door. Or he saw her, and that was what made her look, because otherwise, there wasn't much about him that stood out.

Brown hair—at least he still had his hair, eyes the same color, and lines on his face that made him look older than he was. Or maybe it was the lack of joy in his face that aged him. What stood out was his intensity. It radiated across the room. She remembered him, too.

She wondered if he remembered her. So yes, he had caught her eye. And, she had to admit, that rarely happened.

Mama and Lizzy nodded yes.

Tom said out loud what she was thinking: "Well, that answers why he is so hyper vigilant. He lost his brother. Do you think he's still looking for him?"

"If anyone still is, it would be Alex," Lizzy answered. "Unless someone finds Zach, we may never know what happened to him."

"Well, if that was the first boy, assuming he didn't leave town on his own—after all, ten years old is awfully young to run away on your own—who was next?" Serenity asked.

"Five years later, another boy went missing. Most people had forgotten about Alex's brother by then. Only a few people thought to connect the two. The sheriff, at the time, was a complete idiot. Barely competent to run anything, let alone a search for a missing boy," Mama said, disgust in her voice.

"The truth is, we've had a barely competent sheriff in Lazy Falls for years. It was only when Alex took over that things changed. And that's a good thing too, because drugs have come here just as they have in every town."

Serenity sighed. This is why she had stayed away from people. She didn't want to know about any of this, let alone see memories of it. But she had been wrong. So wrong. If she and her mother had opened themselves up to people and their memories, then they might have been able to stop whatever was happening to the boys.

Serenity glanced at her mother and then at Mama and Tom. All of them stood up as Mama said, "That's enough of that for now. Let's get you back in bed."

Lizzy wanted to protest. They needed to go on and find the latest boy, but she was too tired to get the words out. After Serenity was ensured that her mother was comfortable, she came back to the living room to see Tom and Mama getting ready to leave.

"We have solved nothing," Serenity said. It surprised her that she felt so driven to do something. It had been years since she wanted to do anything but paint by herself, a participant in life as an outside observer.

Mama sighed, put her arm around Serenity, and pulled her close. At first, Serenity resisted. It was hard to let go and be comforted. For a moment, she thought she would break down in tears, but she shut it down as quickly as she could. No time for tears, and besides, Mama and Tom might feel compelled to do something about them.

But she let herself sink into the embrace, smelling the soft scent of someone who worked with dirt and flowers, and smiled at Tom over Mama's shoulder. She had been lucky to have found him as a friend when they were still children. She knew it went both ways, but now that she was home, she could see that she was still the broken one. Tom had grown up and learned how to become part of the world. She had avoided it as much as possible, so truthfully, she hadn't grown up yet.

"Shall I bring Brad over tomorrow?" Tom asked.

"Yes, please. And thank you."

Both Mama and Tom knew she was saying thank you for much more than the upcoming consultation about the house. Tom put his hand out to his mom and helped her down the chipped front porch steps, thinking that the first order of business was finding someone who could repair the house to at least get rid of the hazards.

"One more thing," Serenity called out to them. "Are all the boys that are taken the same?"

"In age, yes." Mama replied. "They are all ten. Including the latest one."

Eighteen

Before heading out for her pre-dawn walk, the one she was determined to do every day, Serenity peaked in at her mother to make sure she was still sleeping and then slipped out the back door.

Although sunrise would not be for another thirty minutes, the sky was light, and the birds were raucous in the trees. She could make out the call of the cardinal, the song of the robin, and the whistle of the chickadee. In the huge thuja that grew along the side of the backyard, a chorus of birds chattered at each other. When she was a child, she imagined the tree as an apartment building, and every morning the residents would fling open their doors and call cheerily out to each other.

"Are you still there?" They'd ask. "How did you sleep? What did you dream about? What are your plans for today? Do you want to play?" She'd laugh at that picture. Birds and their songs had always brought her joy. *How could they not? She* thought. The morning song was a display of community, of being alive together.

Even the "loner" birds had community. The hawk might not be as social as the chickadee or the blue jay, but they still had some kind of community. And even though she had thought she didn't need community, she did. Everyone did. A day with Mama and Tom had shown her what she had been missing.

Before starting her walk, Serenity stood for a moment, surveying the wreck of their backyard. The backyard, which used to be so beautiful, was now overgrown with weeds and littered with limbs from the trees. She could see that Mama had done a little with it the day before, but there was a long way to go before it looked like it used to.

She knew if she turned to look at the house, it would be even worse. It sagged. Just like her. She was only fifty, but she sagged. If she was a yard, she'd be weedy and littered like this one. She wondered if everything was so far gone that it couldn't be fixed. It felt as if the only path she had left open in her life was the one to her painting. When she was in the flow of painting, it was like living in another time zone, another dimension.

Painting for her was an escape from the ugliness in the world. Which was what people felt when they looked at them. And that made her a wealthy painter. She knew she was lucky to have become this successful. She could remain private and untouchable while making a difference in people's lives.

She didn't want to pull down the wall she had so carefully constructed around herself entirely, but at the same time, she knew she needed to become more present in this world. It had helped to spend the time with Tom and Mama. They had made peace with themselves and the world and found a way to exist within it. She could do the same thing. Somehow.

Picking her way around the house, using the old stone path that was barely visible, she stood at the front of the house and breathed in the surroundings. She always had a keen sense of smell. She knew that smell triggered memories, and she often smelled something before she saw someone else's memory.

Despite that, she loved that she could easily smell the depth of the earth, the leaves as she stepped on them, the hint of rain. The leaves rustled, and she watched as a skunk walked by, ignoring her completely as it headed into the bushes that grew wild on the side of the yard. It pleased her to think that the mess of a yard probably harbored many animals, and she didn't want to disturb the homes. She just wanted a little more order and beauty.

Get going, she said to herself and started off down the lane towards the road. For someone who could always see what needed to be made better, it was amazing how she had ignored what was right in front of her. Herself. At first her hips and calves hurt so much she was gritting her teeth as she walked, a little moan escaping once in a while.

But sooner than she had thought possible, they relaxed, and the walk became easier than it had been just the day before. It was hard to believe that at one time she'd run down this road, but she had. And she'd do it again. First walk, then jog, then see if she could actually break out into a run. She'd never be twenty again, but she could be a healthy fifty years old. That was young in today's world.

A car came toward her, and she stepped off the road to let it pass, grateful that whoever was driving saw her and swerved to her right a little. She raised her hand in thanks, and whomever it was, in the car returned the wave. Serenity smiled to herself, thinking that it was like one bird calling to another. She didn't know who had been in the car, but they had acknowledged each other's presence. A small evidence of community.

It had always scared her how many people saw nothing other than what was visible through the tunnel vision of what was in front of them. It was why she walked facing traffic. She couldn't count on being seen as she walked. She had heard too many stories of unseeing drivers hitting people from behind.

Tunnel vision was dangerous. It kept people from knowing each other, appreciating their differences, and acknowledging how connected everyone was. A bird couldn't afford tunnel vision. For them, it was a death sentence. Perhaps it was for humans, too. But she couldn't hate people for choosing it. After all, it was what she, her mother, and her daughter had practiced. Heck, it was what all the Rivers women practiced, at least as far back as she knew. They thought it made them safe, but in reality, it made them easy prey.

The reality of what that meant took her breath away. They had been lucky so far, living in their protected shells. But how long would that luck last? It was time to open up to the world and be of service. Serenity wondered if she practiced, if she could become better at choosing what memories to see. Because if she could do that, she might see something that would lead to solving the mystery of the missing boys.

And right now there was a boy missing. She hoped he had only run away. And maybe if she met the parents, she could see a memory that would help. One they might not know was important or had forgotten.

As she walked, Serenity thought about how she might learn how to handle seeing something that people mostly didn't want anyone to see—things she didn't want to see, either. But perhaps she could learn how to deal with them and maybe help her mother and daughter at the same time.

But even if it was hard for her to do it, it was time to learn how to use her gift and be grateful for it. It wasn't about her and what she wanted. It was about a boy who needed to be found.

Nineteen

Serenity glanced at her watch. It was time. Her plan was to walk five minutes more each day before turning around. Looking both ways, she crossed the road to return home, proud of herself. Not only had she gone five minutes longer, she wasn't as tired as she was before. *I'll be running in no time*, she thought, and then laughed at herself. She was making progress, but it would be a while before she started running. She would be lucky to be jogging a few steps or two.

As she made the turn toward home, she caught a smell of car exhaust, but not seeing or hearing a car realized it might be a memory. But whose? She had her answer as a lone male runner passed her. He grunted and waved and ran on. Not a jogger, a runner. She didn't know who he was, and she hoped he didn't know her either. She had her hair pulled back in a ponytail threaded through a plain blue baseball hat.

She let herself see the memory as he passed, trying to control the intensity of it, hoping she could make it like watching TV in the background with the sound turned way down. That's the image she kept in her head as she watched a memory of being in a car racing down a street, or road, or track?

Either way, it had worked. She barely saw it and only felt the faintest of emotions. Maybe a little joy at how fast the car had been going and some regret over something that had happened that kept him from doing that again. It only took a few seconds for the memory to flash through, and another to cleanse herself of it. She assigned it to a place in her head, called other people's memories, and then shut her mental door on it.

Phew, that wasn't bad, Serenity thought. *Perhaps it was possible to contain the effects.* By the time she returned home, she had almost convinced herself that she wouldn't mind memory-seeking. Plus, she had an idea for a new painting, and she was only half as exhausted as the day before. It was a good morning.

As she rounded the curve in the lane to the house, she saw Mama's truck and a truck with the sign Tate's Nursery parked in front. Fear rushed through her. Did something happen to her mother? She quickened her steps and rushed into the house, only calming down when she saw her mother dressed and sitting at the kitchen table, smiling at her, with a piece of half-eaten toast in front of her.

Mama was sitting at the table with Brad. Calming her heart, Serenity smiled at the three of them, as if she hadn't been scared out of her mind just a moment before.

"Sit," Mama said.

Pouring herself a cup of coffee, Serenity took a seat beside the man and said, "Thanks for coming, Brad. We didn't get to talk when I saw you yesterday."

"I'm happy to be here. Tom has told me all about what a good friend you have been to him through the years."

"It's easy to be friends with him," Serenity answered.

Brad smiled, a smile that lit up his face and crinkled his eyes. Serenity decided that Brad matched his name. He was taller than Tom, with dark hair gone gray, but that made him even more ruggedly good-looking while still appearing gentle. Few people could pull that off. She decided that Tom and Mama were quite safe with Brad around.

She wanted to thoroughly question Brad, starting with where he and Tom met, but Mama obviously had other plans.

"I'm not going to beat around the bush," she said. Serenity and Lizzy looked at each other. When had Mama not been direct?

"Brad here is going to be in charge of fixing up this wreck of a house," she paused long enough to give Lizzy the chance to disagree or be mad, but Lizzy did neither.

"But it is going to be an enormous mess while it's happening. So we've decided you, Lizzy, will come live with me in the meantime."

"Oh no," Lizzy said. "No way."

"Sorry, you don't have a choice. I have a beautiful room for you to stay in, and one for Serenity too, if she wants to come. But I know your daughter will agree that a construction zone is no place for you to live. Brad knows a team that will get most of the work done quickly, and then we can discuss you moving back as they finish up."

Mama looked up over at Serenity. "You agree, don't you?"

Seeing the look on Mama Tate's face, Serenity knew she didn't have a choice. Besides, when she thought about it, she realized it would be much easier to get everything done if no one had to worry about how her mother was feeling.

"I do. It's for the best mom. Besides, you and Mama can get into all sorts of trouble together. And perhaps Tom wouldn't mind you helping at the nursery. It will be good for you."

Lizzy thought about what she had promised herself. That she would help her daughter and hopefully her granddaughter learn how to use their gift and not run away from it as she had done. Mama was giving her the perfect way for her to ease herself back into life. She didn't like it, but she'd do it.

Composing herself so she didn't give away how afraid she was, although Mama probably knew that already, she agreed.

"Let's get you packed up then," Mama said. "We brought a few suitcases, assuming you didn't have any."

That's when Serenity noticed the two suitcases by the front door. Thoughtful. Because Mama was right, there was no way her mother had suitcases. Had she ever traveled anywhere? It was only then that Serenity fully realized how isolated her mother had lived her life.

"Are you coming?" Mama asked Serenity. The way she asked, Serenity knew that even if she wanted to go, it's not what Mama wanted.

"Perhaps I'll stay once in a while at your house, but I think someone needs to stay at our house."

Mama's slight nod to her confirmed she had made the right decision.

The three of them worked together to get Lizzy packed, so she was ready in no time at all. Lizzy thought it was all moving too fast, but that was probably what Mama intended. No time for her to change her mind. Brad said he would be along shortly, but he wanted to talk to Serenity about what needed to be done at the house.

As Mama drove Lizzy away, she turned back to wave, astonished at how bad the house and the grounds looked.

"That's embarrassing," she said, knowing Mama would know what she meant.

"Not going to disagree, Lizzy, but you are doing something about it now. No point living in the past. Time to move forward.

And you have got to stop this 'I'm going to die any minute' crap, too."

The truck bounced and rattled down the lane, only calming down as they hit the road towards the nursery.

"Okay," Lizzy said.

She meant it, but her heart was racing. She had made herself sick so Serenity would come home; could she undo it now, or was it too late?

"Oh, I forgot to tell Serenity something." Mama picked up her phone and said, "Call Serenity."

When Serenity picked up, Lizzy could hear the discussion in the truck. *What kind of magic is this?* She thought. She'd obviously missed out on a few things.

"Forgot to tell you. I made an appointment for you and Tom to see Alex later this morning."

There was a long silence as Serenity realized what Mama wanted her to do. She squeezed her eyes shut, imagining how bad this could be. Brad reached out and touched her shoulder. She shuddered inside but squeezed out the word, "Okay."

What she had said she wanted was happening, and now there was no way to stop it.

Twenty

After walking the entire house with Brad, making notes about everything that needed to be fixed, and Brad snapping pictures along the way, Serenity couldn't decide if she was elated or exhausted. She loved the process of making things better, but this was an enormous project. Much bigger than she had thought it was going to be. Mama Tate was wise to take her mother away.

As they toured the house, Serenity was glad that she had changed her mind about where she wanted her studio. It would be lovely to be able to walk outside rather than coming down the stairs. The room at the back of the house underneath her old bedroom would be perfect. Most of the windows needed to be replaced, so she was going to have one turned into a sliding glass door so she could step outside into the backyard. Which led them to a discussion of a patio and an overhang and a complete overhaul of the garden.

"This is going to be a hugely expensive project," Brad said.

"I have the money." Serenity replied. "Been saving for something. I guess it's this."

Since they had time and Serenity didn't have much with her, the two of them moved her into a small room that would be the last to be updated. And then Brad set up a meeting with the construction crew he wanted to use. After Brad left for the nursery, Serenity sat on a rickety old chair at the edge of the weed garden and called the moving company to find out when the contents of the house she had just sold would arrive. She was assured that it would be by the end of the week.

Which meant she had to figure out where to put all of it. Most of what was coming were her painting supplies. She kept only a few favorite pieces of furniture, including her bed, which she missed terribly. She'd been having a hard time sleeping, which she blamed on the bed she was sleeping on. Her childhood bed. It seemed as if all the memories of not fitting in as a child and the fear of other people's memories seeped into her bones every night. She hated it so much she thought of getting a cot and sleeping on that. Even the floor would be better.

Brad had already arranged for a dumpster to be delivered to the house, and she decided to have them add her old bed to what they were throwing away. The thought of going through the house and ridding it of anything useless or anxiety-producing sounded fun. She was sure that was also part of Mama's intention when she took

Lizzy away from the house. She expected Serenity to rid it of the old and make it livable again. *Mama is a wise woman,* Serenity muttered to herself.

All the details of moving and storing and fixing up swam around in her head, a mix of excitement and worry. But mostly she allowed it to be a distraction. She was nervous about seeing Alex Williams. She had never officially met Alex Williams in person, but she always knew who he was. Who didn't? He had the reputation of a steely, single-minded man. Well, boy, since she hadn't seen him since she left town.

And even then, it had always been from a distance. He was always alone, but there always seemed to be people around him, which, of course, made no sense. Was he always alone, or were people always around him? What she remembered about him, besides the sense that he challenged the world, was a tallish average-looking boy, five years older than her, with brown hair and a determined air about him.

At the diner, she had seen that same determination in him, maybe even more so. Perhaps that came from being the youngest boy in that weird family. Or maybe he had that air about him because his brother went missing, and his older brothers and sisters either died or left town as soon as they were able. She knew that in the end he was the only one left with a mean father, and after his long-suffering mother died, what had that done to him?

Why become a police chief? Why stay in town? Why not run away the same way that she did? But then she came back anyway. Perhaps he had more courage than she did. The truth was, she was anxious about their meeting. It would signal her agreement to get involved with looking for the missing boy and getting caught up in the decades-old mystery about where all the boys went.

It would mean letting in memories and keeping them instead of pushing them into the room in her mind. It would mean sifting through what was relevant and what wasn't. It would mean visiting people in their homes, something she dreaded.

Being in someone else's home meant she could feel their lives. It wasn't just the visual of what was in their homes; it was the emotions and thoughts that had become part of the walls and furniture. She could ask if they could meet at a more common space, but then she might miss out on information that would help find the boy.

It was surprising that places where more people went, like restaurants, were not as bad as where people lived. Probably because so many people went there, they overlaid each other so not one thing stood out, except maybe the overall feel of the place. She always had to stand outside something and wait to be sure she wanted to go in.

But unless you knew her well, you couldn't tell she did it. It was another reason she dreaded meeting Alex Williams. How would the police station feel? But what she was really worried about was meeting the police chief, and she couldn't figure out why it was producing so much anxiety for her.

As she sat in the garden chair, the singing of the birds and the subtle humming of bees dipping in and out of the wild petunias calmed her enough that she fell asleep and dreamed. It was only a swirl of colors. Almost like her paintings, except that she kept thinking that someone was stepping in and out of the swirl.

When she woke, she made a note to try painting what she saw and felt as soon as she had her studio set up again. She'd have to have that room done first; it was already too many days without her art to steady herself. Besides, she had a showing coming up in a few months, and although most of it was done and already in her agent's hands, she needed a few more pieces to round it out. Perhaps what she had just seen in her dream would do it.

Gathering herself, she brushed her teeth and her hair and put on a little eye makeup and sunscreen. At the last minute, she changed her clothes. Jeans, a white blouse, and a light jacket. Hoping for the best, she drove to the station, grateful that Tom would be there too. He was waiting outside for her.

"Are you ready?" He asked. She knew what he was asking. Was she?

"Not really. But we have to do this, anyway."

"Agreed," Tom said as he opened the door and waited for the moment Serenity needed to let everything inside the room wash past her. Although he didn't have her gifts, he could almost feel the flood of emotions that swished around and then drifted past them and out the door.

Serenity nodded her thanks, and they turned together to face what came next.

Twenty One

Sam rolled over, groaned, opened her eyes, and for a minute tried to remember where she was. In her dream, she was in her grandmother's house in an old bedroom tucked in the corner of the upstairs. Her mom had done her best to make it a cozy place for her; her pink bunny with the floppy ears had come with her from home and was tucked under the covers, his head just peeking out from the quilt that had probably been her great-grandmothers.

She had hated and loved that house. It was old. Even as a child, she loved new. She loved the clean, clear lines of a room with hardly anything in it. Muted colors. Some flowers maybe. But not the flowered wallpaper that reminded her of an Agatha Christie story about the flowers turning colors because of poison in the air.

Her mother liked the same thing, so wherever they moved to, it had been cleared, cleaned, and updated, even if it wasn't their house. For a long time, it seemed as if they were always moving.

Her mom would see a memory, and if it was too much for her, they would move on. She had hated the constant moving; she'd just get settled in and they would move again.

But that restlessness seemed to have permeated her life, too. After moving out at eighteen, she had wandered the world, mainly to get away from her mother and what she thought her mother wanted her to be. She spent a few years working odd jobs, getting in trouble, happy no one knew what she was doing. Looking for something. A friend had suggested once that she was looking for her father. That was possible. But since she knew nothing about him, he'd be hard to find. And why would she want to find someone who had abandoned her?

But she had also loved that house. The history of all the women who had lived there seeped into the walls. No memories, though. The house was cleared of memories by each woman so that they could live there. Too bad her mother hadn't figured out how to do that with all the houses they had lived in. Perhaps they wouldn't have moved as much.

The old house was just another reason she wasn't excited about going back there. She had fled Lazy Rivers and come to Spring Falls because she wasn't ready to see her family yet. Which was why she was in a motel. As motels went, it wasn't bad. But it wasn't home. Not that she was clear about what home looked like.

She rolled over, wishing that her pink bunny was really lying beside her, its embroidered blue eyes looking up at her. But of course, that was a dream, and she figured he was long gone. His name had been just Bunny until she read a book called *Watership Down* and called him Bunny Fiver. After all, it was about Fiver, a young rabbit with extrasensory perception. That certainly fit into her life.

Books. Her safe home. Reading took her away from regular life and into other lands and places. She met people she'd never know in real life. She visited lands that someone else imagined, and all of it was like reading memories. But safe ones. It was just a book. Someone else's memory was life.

When she first checked into the motel, a bland young man, glasses and hair pulled back into a ponytail on his neck, seemed boring enough, except she saw a memory of him racing motorcycles on a dirt road, careening off the road and breaking a leg. The memory made her flinch, and a pain shot up her leg, and she had to stop herself from asking him if he was alright. She already knew he wasn't. He was afraid to ride again, and now he was bored and lonely.

As she signed the roster, she mentioned she had just been in Italy and had watched part of the MotoGP. "I'd be afraid, but it looked so exciting," she had said. It was all lies. She knew nothing about it but had seen it flash by on her newsfeed a few days before. He had glanced up at her, a brief spark of interest sparked in his eyes, and before it could go out, she asked if he rode. "Used to," he said, looking down, dull eyes once again.

"Well, I bet you were good at it; if I knew how to ride, I'd definitely not give it up."

All lies. For her, there was no way she was going to get on a motorcycle and go careening down any road. But she wasn't lying for her gain. She was lying to bring him back to life in some small way. To her, they were not the same. She told him a story, hoping it would help. It's what she did. Tell stories. Maybe to bring people back to life or assure them they weren't alone. Or assure herself she wasn't alone.

As a child, she told stories to Bunny Fiver. She'd whisper them to him, and he'd listen and approve. Her mother painted stories—well, not stories, feelings. Her mother painted feelings, and people made up stories about what they felt. She told stories with words, and people made up how they felt about them.

Groaning again, Sam rolled over and pulled the covers up over her head. She loved her mother, even if she spent most of her life angry at her. She even loved her grandmother and her weird old house. But she didn't love the legacy of the Rivers women. If it wasn't for the fact that her grandmother was very ill, she wouldn't have come.

How many more days would she stay away? Maybe one more day. Write a few more chapters in the book. Go out for lunch. Maybe even visit the gallery she had seen. It would be weird if her mother's pictures were already there. But if not, she could tell her about it. And she decided to walk to the campus. Something she and her mother used to do when they visited. They'd drive up from Lazy Rivers and spend part of the day in Spring Falls. They always walked the campus. Now she wondered why. It was pretty, but not that pretty. Had her mother gone to school there? If she had, she never said. Or she never asked.

Her mother. She missed her. They used to have fun together, and then they didn't. Her mom always needed to make things better, and that often felt as if that included making her better. And as she got older, that just didn't sit well. She was herself. She wanted to be herself, different. Not just because she saw people's memories, but because she didn't want to be like everyone else.

But now she wondered if she had rebelled over the wrong thing. For a minute she thought about the eyes in the truck mirror back in Lazy Rivers. If she told herself the truth, she had not only run away from seeing her mother and grandmother but also from the man in the truck. *This is beyond stupid*, she thought. *You are stupid*, she heard in her head. *You're still in bed, you ran away, and you get sad and depressed over nothing.*

"Shut up," she said to that voice. She had stuff to do, and she wasn't stupid. Or lazy. She had been tired. Now she needed coffee, and she knew there was some in the lobby. Sam threw on a pair of sweatpants and top, brushed her hair, slapped some expensive face cream on, made a few faces in the mirror to wake up her face, and headed to the lobby.

There was only one other person there. An older man with gray hair was pouring himself a cup of coffee. When he turned to say hello, she thought, *What a nice man*, and had then thought that he had the same color blue eyes as her mother. Yep, one more day in Spring Falls, and then it was time to go to Lazy Rivers and face her mother.

"Have a nice day," the man said. "You, too," Sam answered, and wondered why the man seemed familiar. *It was just the eyes*, she decided.

Twenty Two

As he finished up repairing a living room wall, Randy thought over his talk with Pete the day before. He had told him about the wall he was fixing because the homeowner's son had gotten angry and punched it. He had broken his hand.

"What was he mad about?" Randy had asked his mother.

"Living here," was her reply, and as she walked away, Randy thought he heard her mumble, "Who can blame him?"

What she meant by that worried him. The house was nice enough; someone took good care of it. After all, they immediately called him to patch the wall. The woman was pretty, but looked tired. Dark rings under her eyes told him she wasn't sleeping well. Although he knew it wasn't any of his business, he made a mental note to check back on her in a few weeks just to make sure that she and her son were okay. He didn't know her husband, but thought he'd ask Pete next time he saw him.

Pete, the initially reluctant conveyor of information about the town, had been good to talk to. Even though Betty Jean had introduced them, Pete had been slow to talk. But once he got Pete talking, he had been highly entertaining and informative. One thing Randy knew how to do was ask questions. It was helpful in his work. It helped him figure out what people really wanted, which was often not what they thought they wanted.

He thought of it like pumping water from a well. Eventually, it gave you what you wanted. It just required a little priming and patience. So, even though he was most interested in the missing boys, he asked instead about Pete's farm. He learned more about farming in the next thirty minutes than he thought possible.

After that, it was easy to get Pete to tell him more about Lazy Rivers, and he didn't have to ask questions anymore. Pete was on a roll. He'd bought Pete another coffee, and they moved to a booth, and Pete became a fount of information. Pete knew everything and everyone. He told Randy who lived where and for how long. He gave Randy a brief history of the town and what it had been like to live there. Eventually he began speculating about what would happen to the town now that new people were moving in who wanted a small town life and could still work thanks to the internet.

Plus, some of the people who grew up in Lazy Rivers were returning home. That's when Randy learned about the Rivers women. From Pete's point of view, they were a strange bunch. They owned the land next to his farm, but he barely ever saw them.

They kept to themselves for the most part, and then when the daughter moved away, he saw her mother even less.

"It's a damn shame," Pete said. "That land has gone to weeds and brush. It's lain fallow since long before I was born. But Elizabeth Rivers hasn't done anything to make it better.

"Could change now though," Pete had said, slurping his coffee, his hand shaking as he put it back in the saucer.

Randy made another note to himself to stop by Pete's farm to check up on him. He knew Pete's wife had died years before and his boys had moved away. Maybe he'd find out from Betty Jean how much help Pete needed. The shaking hands worried him. Pulling himself back to the present, he had asked Pete why things might change now.

"The daughter has come home. I seen her walking down the road the other day. I waved, but I'm sure she didn't know who it was. Sides, I was driving my wife's old car, not a truck, so that wouldn't have helped. Good thing I can see well, 'cause it was still kinda dark out. She was probably trying to avoid being seen around."

When he had asked Pete why that would be the case, Pete leaned in and whispered, "The Rivers women are a strange bunch. See things, they do."

At that, Pete was done talking. Sucking his teeth, he stood and said he had work to do.

"Stop by sometime. I'll show you around."

Randy said he'd be delighted and then sat for a few minutes more with his coffee. It was Betty Jean who filled in a few more details about the Rivers women. From her, he had learned that the woman he had seen with Tom earlier in the diner was the daughter of Elizabeth Rivers.

"Elizabeth's nickname is Lizzy, but when we were kids, we called her Lazy. Like the town. Like the river. We weren't nice to her. Kids can be so mean. But mostly we stayed away from her. Or she stayed away from us."

"Why?"

Betty Jean looked around, and seeing that Joseph was no longer filling the doorway with his presence, sat down and leaned closer to Randy.

"All those Rivers women see memories."

That's as far as she got before Joseph appeared in the doorway again and waved his hand at her to come talk to him. Winking at Randy as she scooped up the empty cups and plates on the table, she added, "And there's another one of them. Serenity's daughter. Think her name is Samantha. Sam. Haven't seen her around since she was a kid. But who knows, maybe they're all coming back."

After that, Randy had gone home, grabbed a beer, and settled down in front of the TV and tried to give his body and mind a rest. It had worked. He fell asleep in the chair and woke up only long enough to drag himself to bed, only bothering to take off his shoes.

Now as he finished up mudding over the new dry wall—he would come back in the morning after it dried to sand and paint it—he thought again of the woman he had briefly glimpsed a few days before. Was it possible she was Serenity's daughter? If so, why hadn't either Pete or Betty Jean seen her? Perhaps it had been a dream.

As he thought about how he could possibly find out and wondered where she had gone, his phone rang.

"Hey Brad," he said, "I was just thinking about you. I wanted to thank you for the work you did on that yard."

"Sure thing. I called to ask if you could stop by the nursery? I have another job for you. You'd have to work with another construction crew. It's a big job. But they could use you."

"Of course," he answered. "I'm open. Where is it?"

When Brad said that it was a house and yard outside of town and that it belonged to a woman named Elizabeth Rivers, Randy decided that the world was working in his favor. Now he could find out for himself if that woman he had seen was a Rivers. Besides, how interesting would it be to work for women who could see memories? He supposed that could be a bad thing, but it could also be quite useful.

Maybe they could help find out what happened to the missing boys. He knew he should probably leave that idea alone; after all, many people were looking for him, but he couldn't stop thinking about it. That, combined with his curiosity about the Rivers women and perhaps the youngest daughter, made him think of his dad. Maybe he could convince him to move to Lazy Rivers. Because at the moment he had no plans to leave. It was just getting interesting.

Twenty Three

The police station was nothing special. Just one small room, and a window cut into the wall with a woman sitting behind it. Serenity could see that there was a way for the woman to pull a glass partition across the opening if she needed to. But now it was wide open and the woman was relaxed as she asked what she could do for them.

"We came to speak to Alex," Tom said.

"About? He's pretty busy right now."

"I imagine he is. That's what we came to speak to him about. Would you tell him that Tom Tate and Serenity Rivers are here to talk to him about the missing boy."

If Serenity wasn't used to people reacting to her name, she might have missed it, but the women's unconscious flinch when Tom said her name was something she had seen before. Sometimes people didn't even try to hide it. But this woman corrected it immediately, and she was sure that Tom didn't notice. Or maybe he did. He knew that the Rivers women were novelties.

The young woman pushed a button, turned away from them, bent her head down and whispered into the phone. Serenity imagined she said something like, "You won't believe who's here."

After hanging up, she smiled and walked around to the wall and unlocked the door to let them in. Pointing to the end of the hall, she said, "His office is down there."

It was a short hallway, and most of the wall was covered with multiple pictures of police officers. Serenity recognized the past police chief. She wondered if you had to die to get on the wall. Alex was standing in the doorway waiting for them. Unsmiling as usual.

"Saw you at the diner. Wasn't completely sure it was you."

"You did, and it was," Serenity answered.

There was a long pause as the two of them looked at each other. Finally Tom asked, "So can we come in?"

Alex stepped back and waved them in without taking his eyes off of Serenity.

"What's wrong with you?" Tom asked, as they sat down across the desk from him. Alex's unwavering gaze on Serenity was making him angry, or nervous. He wasn't sure which one.

"Guess I never thought one of the witches would come see me."

Tom made a motion to stand up, but Serenity put a restraining hand on his arm. She smiled at Alex. It was hard to stay focused because there was one of his memories tugging at edges of her mind.

"Is that because you were afraid of us, or because you wanted to know us."

For a moment, a smile formed at the edge of his mouth, and even though he stopped it, the interest in his eyes gave him away.

"Both, I suppose. And now you've come to see me why?"

"Well, for the same reason you called me a witch, something you know perfectly well is not true. But I can see memories. Sometimes on purpose. Which means I would like to help you find the missing boy."

"So what they say about you is true, then."

"If they say that River's women see memories, then yes, that's true. What else they say is up for dispute."

Alex's brown eyes narrowed, and lines appeared between his eyes as he frowned. Serenity knew what he was thinking, and she agreed.

"You're right Alex. It's not a fun gift to have. But I have it. I'd like to use it if I can to do some good."

"I remember you. You stayed away from everyone. So now you want to come forward and help? Your mother is a recluse. In fact, all you Rivers women stayed away from all of us. Why help now? And besides, perhaps this memories stuff is just a crock of made up lies."

Serenity sighed. "You're right, we did. And now we've decided that was wrong. And as far as whether it's lies or not, why would we make up something that made us pariahs everywhere we went? You remember me, and I remember you. I would see you as you waited for the bus stop. Even though you seemed so still, you were always aware of what was around you. I suppose it comes from being the youngest in a family where at any moment someone would sneak up on you, and never in fun."

"You guessed that."

Serenity closed her eyes and let in the memory that was tugging at her. First, the smell of a musty home. Then, his memory of his brothers coming up behind him and hitting him on the head with his baseball bat, and then taking the new baseball glove he had just earned by working on the farm next door.

"Did you ever get your baseball glove back after your brother hit you with his baseball bat?"

Tom watched Alex take in what she said, wondering if it was a lucky guess. When Serenity added that he had burned his initials into the glove using hot matches, Alex sighed, and Tom caught a moment of fear in his eyes.

But then, who wouldn't be afraid? Here was a woman who could see your lies, even the ones you told yourself. Especially the ones you told yourself.

"Now I see why no one wants the Rivers women around."

Serenity waited.

"But it could come in handy. I'm heading over to see the family. Would you like to come along? I'll say you are a police consultant. Times have changed. We have used strange people like you before."

Serenity tried not to react, to be offended, and then reached over once again to keep Tom from reacting. What good would it do? Alex could call her strange all he wanted, which in fact she was, but she wanted to help. Finally.

"Okay."

"Let's go. They're expecting me. In fact, both of you come. I remember you too, Tom. Another outcast, but for a different reason. Maybe you will hear something the rest of us don't. Besides, you seem to make an excellent guard dog for this one," he said, pointing at Serenity.

"You make it easy to not be liked," Tom said quietly to Alex once Serenity had gone through the door. And then added, "But you are easy to see through, too."

Alex stared at Tom, and then nodded, fully aware that he had opened a door he might not be able to shut again. Life was hard. People were cruel. But here were two people who may make him see it differently.

He wasn't sure if he was more afraid, angry, or hopeful that it would work. He supposed if anyone could push him over the edge one way or another, it would be that woman. He was afraid to say her name, even to himself.

He wondered how easy it would be for him to hide his own memories from her now that he knew it was true that she saw them. Yes. He got his baseball mitt back from his brother. It was the first time, but not the last, that he had stood up to him. It was interesting that she saw one of the pivotal moments of his life.

He'd do his best to hide the other ones, but at the same time hoped that she would help him find the missing boy. He had promised himself that no more kids would go missing while he was sheriff, and then it happened. Again.

If she and her guard dog Tom could help, he'd let them. But that didn't mean he'd let them into his life. He was aware that he was probably telling himself a lie. But for now, he'd let it stand.

Twenty Four

It had taken Matthew a full day to get to Spring Falls. He had forgotten how far it was, or maybe it was because he was getting old, and one hour driving felt like two. *But I'm not too old yet,* he told himself. Only seventy-three. If all went well, he had a good twenty years left to live a good life.

But he had to admit there were things he couldn't do all that well anymore. Like drive all day. When he reached Spring Falls, he had checked into the motel, grabbed a bag of chips from the vending machine, and went straight to bed. After a good night's sleep, he was feeling much better.

While he drove, he had listened to podcasts. They kept him alert as he thought about all the ideas he heard. When he was a child, he had decided he'd not turn into his grandparents. They were lovely people, but so closed off from the world that they barely knew what was happening outside their home. Every year they closed down more, so by the time they died, to him they felt barely present.

No, he had decided. *He'd see the world. He'd learn until he was dead.* It was one reason he had become a journalist. There was a constant influx of ideas and situations to deal with. And just because the newspaper let him go didn't mean he'd have to let himself go. So podcasts told him about human nature, the world, and new ideas kept him company while he drove. He had recorded a few notes on his phone as he drove and he was itching to get to them.

But first he needed coffee, then he'd write for a few hours, and after that go to lunch. He wasn't ready to post anything yet, but writing always cleared his head. After eating, perhaps he'd take a walk around the campus. Let memories fill his head and see where that took him. After that, he'd have to decide how long he'd stay in Spring Falls before driving to Lazy Rivers.

He could pretend all he wanted to that he wasn't going to go, but of course he would, although he'd have to gather up a lot of courage to do it. It didn't matter if Elizabeth was dead or alive; either way, he'd be devastated. But this living in limbo was ridiculous.

The girl getting coffee in the lobby had startled him. She was so young and beautiful. Long dark hair, and if his eyesight hadn't failed him, dark green eyes. She reminded him of a monarch butterfly. Bright, full of life, and yet secretive. Being a journalist, he read people without even thinking about it. He was always looking for interesting people to talk to, so seeing someone like her in a motel lobby intrigued him.

Besides, in that moment when they saw each other, he felt as if he knew her. Which was ridiculous, to say the least. How could he? He watched her go, trying not to stare. She didn't turn around, so either she hadn't noticed him, didn't care, or was good at not showing her curiosity.

After she left, he asked the clerk behind the counter what was a good restaurant to go to for lunch. Looking up, the guy barely registered that he was there, but said there was a good one downtown called ParaTi's. Then, eyes glazed over, looked back at his phone. Matthew had a quick look at a video game.

That was another way to shut down from life, he thought. He loved his phone, but was careful to not let it distract him from reality. Of course, Matthew was fully aware that reality was not the reality—it was a reality. Based on what, he wasn't sure since he had no hard evidence. But he knew there couldn't be only one so-called reality. He had too many strange experiences to think otherwise. Were there parallel universes that sometimes bumped into each other's time lines? Possibly.

His favorite college teacher had often talked about time. Was it a river, and you could only go with the flow? Was it a construct of memories that changed when you thought about it? Was it circular, repeating itself over and over again. Was it none of those things, just an invention to keep us grounded? Or maybe all of them. Elizabeth Rivers had made him think that time might be just a collection of memories. But did that make it any less real? She was as real to him now as she was over fifty years before.

He had been a brand new idea in the world when they met—ready to discover everything. But after meeting Lizzy, he had decided that Lazy Rivers might be just enough for him. She had decided differently and pushed him away and made him promise to never come back.

But those six months had changed his entire view of the world. He had kept his promise, and now he was going to break it. As worried as he was about what he would find, he was sure she was still alive. His heart would be broken if she wasn't. Sure, there had been multiple relationships in his life, some longer than others. Some he had even loved. But none of them had been Elizabeth Rivers.

When he would go to Lazy Rivers, he wasn't sure. He just knew that he would because now he was less than a few hours away, so he'd let himself think about it a little longer. He thought his plan to do some writing, then some food, was a good one. Plus, hopefully hear some good gossip to fuel his imagination. After that, a walk would clear his head, and he would listen for new writing ideas.

Heading back to his room, he looked for the woman butterfly. He wanted to see her again. But if he had learned anything covering the events of the world, he was not in charge of anything. He was an observer. And more than once he had been given what he needed in the moment if he was willing to wait in expectation of it.

He expected to see her again. And he expected she had something to tell him. What it was, he didn't know. In the meantime, he had plenty to write about, and he knew that once he started, he would have more. A long time ago, he had learned that the act of starting something opened a door to more. Writing was definitely like that. He'd swear he had nothing to say, but once he started writing, more ideas flowed in. Matthew thought all of life was like that; until you made a decision and took some action, nothing happened.

It wasn't as if he always knew what he'd write or what life would bring. In fact, he rarely did. But he trusted that in the end, it would be a good thing. Not always at first, but the key was to not stop, evaluate yes, make new choices yes, but not stop.

That's how he knew for sure he'd be heading to Lazy Rivers soon. He couldn't stop what he had started.

Twenty Five

They went in separate cars. Alex wanted them all to pile into his, but Serenity refused. She could have gone with Tom, but on the other hand, she couldn't bring herself to do it. She kept envisioning that she would need to run out of the house, get into a car, and drive away. Tom didn't even blink when she suggested they go separately. Not just because he knew how she felt, but because he felt the same way. *What if he needed to escape?*

The heat outside was oppressive. It was much too hot for June. But it felt appropriate for what was happening. Everything was pushing, so that nothing was comfortable.

They pulled up to a small house in a neighborhood that lay on the outskirts of town. Although some of the neighboring houses looked neglected, with rusted pieces of equipment as part of the front yard. Posing as art sculptures perhaps, Tom thought, trying to be charitable but being snarky instead. The Hunter's house was well maintained, especially considering their neighbors. A riot of wilted pansies struggled to bloom in a pot by the front door. Who had time to water plants when a son was missing?

Tom and Alex waited for Serenity to get out of her car. They could see her looking out the window as if there was something there to see. There wasn't. Two straggly trees shimmered in the slight breeze, and a few kids flew by on bikes. Finally she sighed and stepped out of the car, shivering as if it were cold, when actually it was stifling. *Without the breeze, the heat would be unbearable,* Tom thought. He knew what she was doing. Calming herself. Hoping she could help and yet hating what she had to do anyway.

Seeing Serenity heading up the driveway, Alex muttered, "Finally," and turned to ring the doorbell. Just as Serenity reached the door, it swung open, revealing a girl who looked about six with a gap-toothed smile.

"Mom said, come in," she said, smiling directly at Serenity. The girl reminded her of her daughter, and she smiled back, hoping that whatever memories the girl had were good ones. Tom kept his hand on the small of her back, not pushing but gently guiding, and it felt reassuring that he was there. Alex introduced the two of them to the woman and man on the couch, Jimmy's parents.

Serenity thought if they could sit further away from each other, they would. The little girl, who declared her name as Mandy, sat between them. Trying to bridge the gap and failing. The feeling of failure filled the room as if it were a scent clinging to everything.

Serenity sat across from the family, her eyes darting between the parents and Mandy. She could feel the memories pressing against her consciousness, like whispers trying to be heard. She took a deep breath, steeling herself for what was to come. Mr. and Mrs. Hunter sat tensely on the couch, their bodies rigid with worry and exhaustion.

Jack Hunter was a tall, lean man in his early forties. His sun-weathered face spoke of years of working outdoors, likely in construction or farming. Serenity had asked Alex not to tell her anything about the family. She wanted to see and hear it for herself. Deep worry lines creased Jack's forehead, and what was probably always a neatly trimmed beard now looked unkempt. His calloused hands fidgeted restlessly, a stark contrast to his otherwise still demeanor.

To Serenity he looked like a man trying to contain his anger. *But what was he angry about? His son missing? Or was his son missing because of his anger?*

Jimmy's mother, Sarah, was a petite woman with shoulder-length auburn hair that looked like it hadn't been brushed in days. Her green eyes, usually bright and lively according to the memories Serenity glimpsed, were now red-rimmed and puffy from crying. She wore a faded floral blouse and kept twisting a silver locket around her neck—a nervous habit that Serenity sensed was relatively new.

Her daughter, Mandy, looked like her. As they sat, waiting to talk, Serenity pieced together an image from the parents' memories and the photos scattered around the living room of what Jimmy looked like. He was more like his father.

Jimmy was a lanky ten-year-old with a mop of unruly brown hair that constantly fell into his eyes. His face was sprinkled with freckles across the nose and cheeks, giving him a mischievous look that matched the twinkle in his hazel eyes. A photo on the mantel of the family showed him wearing an oversized Little League baseball jersey—number 7—and a gap-toothed grin that mirrored his younger sister's.

A memory pushed itself to Serenity. It was Sarah Hunter's memory of her son on his tenth birthday just a month ago, blowing out candles on a baseball-shaped cake. He was wearing his favorite red sneakers, scuffed at the toes from countless adventures, some of which he had gotten in trouble for because he hadn't said where he was going.

In the few moments since they had arrived, Jimmy became more real, and the need to find him even more urgent to Serenity. He wasn't just another missing child statistic. The weight of her responsibility settled heavily on Serenity's shoulders as she absorbed the family impressions and let herself see a few of their memories. She became even more aware that her gift might be the key to bringing Jimmy back to his family.

"Mr. and Mrs. Hunter," Alex began, his voice softer and kinder than what Serenity expected. "We appreciate you meeting with us again. We know this is difficult, and I know you have told me and my deputies this information before, but these two people, Tom and Serenity, are now working with us, and it would be better if you could tell them yourself about the last time you saw your son."

The mother's eyes welled up with tears, while the father's jaw clenched. Mandy looked up at her parents, then back at Serenity, her gap-toothed smile fading.

"We've told you everything," Mr. Hunter said, his voice strained. "He was playing in the backyard. We checked on him every few minutes. And then... he was just gone."

As he spoke, flashes of memory flickered through Serenity's mind. A boy laughing, running through sprinklers. The same boy, older now, is arguing with his father. Doors slamming. Tears. So much pain and regret.

Serenity blinked, trying to focus on the present. She felt Tom's hand on her arm, grounding her.

"Mrs. Hunter," Serenity asked quietly, "Can you tell me about your son's friends? Anyone he might have gone to see?"

As the mother spoke, more memories flooded Serenity's senses. A group of boys on bikes, riding down a dusty path. An old abandoned house at the edge of town. A strange symbol carved into a tree. Serenity's breath caught in her throat. She'd seen that symbol before, but where? Maybe it was connected to the other boys missing from Lazy Rivers.

"There's an old house," Serenity said, her voice barely above a whisper. "Near the edge of town. Did your son ever mention it?"

Both Alex and Tom looked at Serenity, wondering where she got that information. The parents exchanged a confused look, but Mandy's eyes widened.

"The spooky house!" she exclaimed. "Jimmy said it was haunted. He and his friends were going to explore it, but I told him not to 'cause it's scary."

Alex leaned forward; this was new information for him. "When did Jimmy tell you this, Mandy?"

"Last week," the girl replied, fidgeting with her dress. "He said it was a secret, but I heard him talking to his friends on the phone."

Serenity felt a chill run down her spine, despite the oppressive heat. She knew, with a certainty that came from years of dealing with her gift, that the old house held a key to finding Jimmy and perhaps uncovering the truth about the missing boys of Lazy Rivers.

As they prepared to leave, Serenity caught a last glimpse of a memory—a shadowy figure watching the house from the tree line. She shuddered, realizing that the danger was far from over and that her decision to embrace her ability might have consequences she wasn't prepared for.

But then she knew that already. And it was too late to turn back now.

Twenty Six

Serenity couldn't get home from the Hunter's house fast enough. She had politely thanked them and calmly walked to the car, but inside, Serenity felt overwhelmed as anger, sorrow, and joy mixed into one big, muddy mess. Tom leaned in the car window and said it would be alright. She nodded and smiled at Tom and calmly drove away, although it felt as if the heat was chasing her and the stuffy smell of the Hunter's home clung to her skin.

Alex had asked her to come to the old house with him, but she couldn't. Just couldn't. Not now. Besides, she knew in her gut that Jimmy wasn't there. He had been. But he was gone. Alex could collect his evidence, and she would go there herself once the feeling of total and complete overwhelm subsided. Nothing she did right at that moment was going to change anything, anyway. Of course, she could be wrong. Despite that, there was no way she could do it anymore today.

Before leaving the Hunters, Tom said he was going back to the nursery, careful not to touch her, knowing that one more sensation would probably bring her to her knees. They agreed to talk later. As she made her way home, all she could think about was getting home and falling into bed. Except she had allowed herself to forget that the house was going to be a construction zone. And now there were two trucks in her driveway.

No, no, she said to herself. *I can't.* But there was no choice. There were people there already, and she had nowhere else to go. She recognized the nursery's truck but not the other one. Serenity pulled up behind the unfamiliar truck, her heart sinking. She sat in her car for a moment, trying to gather her strength. The memories from the Hunter house still swirled in her mind, making it hard to focus on the present. It seemed the old fact of one memory a day was over. At least for now.

Taking a deep breath, she stepped out of her car. The heat hit her like a wall, but it was almost a relief compared to the emotional weight she carried. As she approached the house, Brad stepped out onto the front porch, wiping sweat from his brow with the back of his hand. For a second, she had a memory of herself as a child with her mother. They were sitting on the front porch together, watching a herd of deer meander through the yard.

"Serenity!" he called out, a friendly smile on his face. "Hope you don't mind us getting started. Your mom said you'd be okay with it. She said she wants to get home as soon as possible, so go fast were her orders."

Serenity forced a smile, nodding weakly. "Of course, Brad. Thanks for making this happen so quickly."

Just then, another man stepped out onto the porch. He was tall and wiry, brown hair falling into his eyes as he held his cap in his hands. His dark brown eyes crinkled at the edges as he smiled at her.

"This is Randy," Brad introduced him. "He's a handyman around town. I've worked with him before. He'll be my point man with the construction crew. Randy, this is Serenity, the daughter of the homeowner."

Randy extended his hand, then seemed to think better of it since his hands were dirty from poking around in the house and gave a small wave instead. "Nice to meet you, ma'am. I, uh, I think I saw you at the diner yesterday with Tom."

Serenity nodded, trying to keep herself together. She felt so overwhelmed with all that had happened already that day; she wasn't sure if she could keep Randy and Brad's memories at bay, and she was too exhausted to deal with them. But she did her best to let none of her anxiety show.

"Randy's going to be overseeing most of the day-to-day work here," Brad continued, aware of the tension but not knowing what to do about it.

"We've gone through the house together. He's got a clear idea of what is supposed to happen, but he and I will check with you as we go, just to make sure. One good thing, the house has a solid foundation."

Serenity tried to focus on Brad's words, but her attention kept drifting to Randy. There was something about him. Something that she couldn't decide if she liked or not. He felt like a curious cat. Was he always like that, or was she just projecting her own unease?

"That's... that's great," she managed to say. "I appreciate you both getting started so quickly."

"No problem at all," Brad replied cheerfully. "We'll get out of your hair now, but we'll be back bright and early tomorrow to really get things moving."

As the men packed up their tools and prepared to leave, Serenity couldn't shake the feeling that there was more to Randy than met the eye. She watched as he climbed into his truck, his gaze lingering on her for a moment before he drove away.

Once both trucks had disappeared down the street, Serenity let out a long, shaky breath. The day's events had left her drained, and now this additional complication with Randy added another layer of uncertainty to her already chaotic thoughts. She trudged into the house, the familiar creaks of the floorboards a small comfort.

At first she expected her mother's voice to call out, but of course she wasn't there. She was over at Mama Tate's, probably resting, or at least she hoped she was. She envied her.

With Brad and Randy gone, she finally had the house to herself, free to nap. She was hungry, but it would have to wait. After that, she'd call her mom. Find out how she was and tell her about Jimmy, about the old house, and about the strange connection she sensed with Randy.

The mysteries of Lazy Rivers were piling up, and Serenity had a sinking feeling that this was only the beginning.

Twenty Seven

When Tom arrived at the nursery, he found his mother supervising the arrangement of the new plants that had just been unloaded and Lizzy sitting at one of the small tables set around the grounds. The tables had been his grandfather's idea.

He had wanted customers to stay and enjoy the nursery, so he gave them a place to sit and look at the plants rather than rushing around trying to get done. Lizzy was sitting at the table with the bright orange umbrella, looking marginally better than when he had seen her that morning.

"You look relaxed," Tom said, sitting beside her and placing a glass of cold water on the table for her.

"Have you always been this thoughtful?" Lizzy asked.

"Not really. But Brad has brought out the best in me. And your daughter."

"Is she doing okay?"

"Being at the boy's home and talking to his parents was hard for her, but she's determined."

"I wish I could say I had a part in that, but I didn't. She raised herself to be that way. I have always been a coward. I saw how hard life was for my mother and grandmother because of this ridiculous gift, and I wanted no part of it. But now I see what a mistake we have made, all of us Rivers women. We stayed apart from everyone. We didn't develop the ability to exist in the world and be useful."

Tom reached over and took one of Lizzy's hands in his. It was thin and dry, but still beautiful, with long, elegant fingers. The same fingers that Serenity had. He wondered if her daughter had the same ones.

"Have you heard from your granddaughter?"

Lizzy shook her head. "But she's around here somewhere. I can feel her. Probably just unwilling to come back to the house. Looking at Serenity and Sam, I can see so clearly how I failed them both."

Tom took a moment to look over the grounds of the nursery at all the flowers and trees, all in different cycles of growth, before answering.

"Does it matter about that? Doesn't it matter more what's happening now? There are seasons of life. Doesn't the Bible say that? And nature shows us that cycle of life all the time. It all weaves together, doesn't it?"

Pointing to a Mock Orange bush that was bursting with buds and flowers that they could smell from where they sat, he said, "Doesn't it matter more what we are today than even yesterday? A few months ago, there were no leaves on this bush. Look at it today. It's a different bush. Just like you. Today you are blooming. Today, you can have a different relationship with them. Because today you are this person."

Tom hadn't seen his mother coming up behind him as he spoke, but felt her arm on his shoulder as she said, "My son. The philosopher."

He looked up at her and smiled, "I learned from the best, mom."

A rumble of thunder sounded in the distance.

"Let's get home before the storm," Mama said to Lizzy. "We'll have pizza and watch one of those old movies together."

Lizzy's eyes filled with tears. "Like we did when we were kids."

As Mama helped Lizzy to the car, she looked back at Tom and smiled. She had heard what he said about being a new person each day. It had helped her too. She also had regrets. And although she hadn't said anything to anybody yet, her biggest regret was that she hadn't said what she had seen years before when Alex's brother, Zach, went missing.

Perhaps it was nothing, but she had been afraid that it was her fault that it had happened. At least that first time. Maybe it was about Zach, but every boy missing since then? How could that be her fault? And were they connected, or they just looked that way?

As the first drops of rain began to fall, Tom watched his mother's car disappear down the driveway with Lizzy inside. He couldn't shake the feeling that there was more going on with his mother than she was letting on. At the police station with Alex, as they talked about the list of missing boys, starting with Alex's brother, something had stirred in his memory—a long-forgotten conversation overheard as a child, perhaps.

He made his way back to the nursery office as the storm clouds gathered overhead. The air was thick with the scent of rain-soaked earth and blooming flowers, a stark contrast to the heaviness in his heart.

As he opened the office door, his phone buzzed in his pocket. It was a text from Serenity.

"There was a man named Randy at the house today with Brad. He was sitting with Pete at the diner. Do you remember him? Something feels off. Can you come over for coffee in the morning?"

Tom frowned, vaguely remembering the man from the diner. He quickly typed a reply. "Of course. Get some rest."

As the last of the customers ran for their cars, Tom told his staff to head home. He loved being the last person there, making sure everything was safe and tucked in. The night lights and alarms came on automatically as soon as he locked the doors for the night. He always had to suppress the urge to say good night to every plant in the place. It would take hours, so instead he whispered a good night to the nursery, trusting that they all heard him.

He wasn't the first person to say goodnight to them. He had heard his grandfather, his father, and now his mother do the same thing. It was a tradition that he happily cared for.

The rumble of thunder grew louder, and the flash of lightning got closer as Tom got into his truck. He couldn't help but feel that the storm wasn't just in the sky—it was brewing in Lazy Rivers itself, stirring up long-buried secrets and forgotten memories. As he drove home, his mind raced with questions. What had his mother seen all those years ago? Because he knew she had. A long time ago, she had told him she had seen something but hadn't told him what. But both of them had decided it was too late to do anything about it.

But now another boy was missing. How was it connected to Zach's disappearance and the current missing boy, Jimmy? And what role did Randy play in all of this? Or was it something else Serenity was worried about? After all, Randy was much too young to be involved in all the missing boys. Alex had disappeared fifty years ago. A half century. Said that way, it was ancient.

The rain started coming down in sheets, matching the turbulent thoughts in Tom's mind. He gripped the steering wheel tighter, feeling the weight of responsibility pressing down on him. Serenity needed him, and he was determined to be there for her, just as she had always been there for him.

But now he needed to rest the same as she did. In the morning, things might look very different. Whatever storm was coming, they would face it together. Besides, Brad might have some insight they could use. Tom took a deep breath, thinking how much the rain obliterated his ability to see, so he had to reduce his speed to almost a crawl, lights blinking to let people know he was there, and how much the mystery around the missing boys felt the same.

They couldn't see the big picture, and they were moving very slowly. *Better safe than sorry,* popped into his head, and then wondered if little Jimmy was glad they were moving so slowly. Or was he at a place where it didn't matter anymore?

Twenty Eight

Matthew's lunch at ParaTi's was delightful. A lovely young woman waited on him, and the food was delicious. Nearby, a group of five women were sitting together, laughing and talking. He thought they were all beautiful. The waitress saw him staring and asked if he'd like to know who they were. Always interested in other people, he had said yes.

"Well," she said, "the red-haired woman is the new mayor of Spring Falls, Judith Zoe. The woman with the short, dark hair is my mom, Bree Mann. The tall woman and the short woman with fluffy brown hair are Marsha and April. They own the yoga/dance studio a few blocks away. The woman with blond hair laughing with Judith owns the art gallery. The cool part of all of this is that they have all been friends since grade school, and they call themselves the Ruby Sisters."

Matthew only heard part of what she said. Bree Mann was one of his favorite authors and here she was, just a few tables away. Dragging himself away from staring, he said, "And your name?"

"Mary Patterson. Is there anything else I can get you?"

Leaning closer, he whispered, "Next time you talk to your mother, tell her one of her biggest fans was sitting a few tables away."

Mary whispered back, "You could tell her yourself."

"No," Matthew said. "This was enough. It was a lovely lunch. Thank you."

Time for my walk, Matthew said to himself. Glancing at the weather app, he saw a storm system moving in, but he had time for a short walk. He left a generous tip for Mary, took one last look at the five women, and stepped into the heat of the day. The edge of the campus was just a few blocks away, so he took his time, glancing at the store windows. He stood outside the art gallery for a moment admiring what he saw and then turned up into the campus's wide walkway lined with trees.

As he walked, he wondered when he would get himself to go to Lazy Rivers. *Maybe tomorrow,* he thought. He couldn't put it off forever. The campus was cooler, the trees providing plenty of shade, but still the heat of the day pressed down despite the looming storm clouds, or maybe because of them. The campus was quiet. Matthew thought that most students were likely avoiding the oppressive weather by staying inside the air-conditioned rooms. Manicured lawns and neat flower beds lined the walkways, creating a picturesque scene.

As he rounded a corner near the library, he spotted a familiar figure—the young woman he'd seen earlier at the motel, getting coffee. She was sitting on a bench, looking lost in thought. When she looked up and saw Matthew, a flicker of recognition passed over her face.

"Hello again," Matthew said, offering a friendly smile. "Fancy meeting you here."

The young woman—Samantha, though Matthew didn't know her name—returned the smile. "Hi there. Are you a professor here?"

Matthew chuckled. "No, just a visitor enjoying a walk. Mind if I join you?"

Samantha gestured to the space beside her. As Matthew sat down, he felt an inexplicable sense of comfort, as if he'd known this young woman for years.

"So, what brings you to Spring Falls?" Samantha asked.

Matthew paused, weighing his words. "I'm a writer. Actually, a journalist. I used to travel all the time all over the world for stories. Now that I'm retired from that, I'm looking for a way to continue that work on my own and not get bored with life just sitting around."

Samantha's eyes lit up. "A journalist. I love that. But why come here to Spring Falls?"

"I went to school here, and one of my favorite teachers taught here, so as I contemplated a new life, this seemed like a good place to start." Matthew didn't include the fact that he was also there because he was avoiding going to Lazy Rivers.

Samantha chose not to tell Matthew she wrote books. He was still a stranger after all. Instead, she told him she loved to read, so they fell into an easy conversation about books, writing, and the charm of small towns. Samantha's insights and her passion for literature impressed Matthew.

"Are you a student here?" Matthew asked, gesturing to the surrounding campus.

Samantha shook her head. "No, I'm just... visiting. Trying to figure some things out." There was a hint of something—uncertainty, perhaps—in her voice that Matthew couldn't quite place. It felt similar to his own. As they talked, the sky grew darker, and a cool breeze ruffled the leaves of the tree they were sitting under. Matthew glanced at his watch, realizing he'd spent more time chatting than he'd intended.

"I should probably head back before the rain starts," he said, standing up. "It was really nice talking with you."

Samantha nodded, smiling. "Likewise. Maybe I'll see you around town. Or the motel even!"

They both laughed as Matthew rose to leave. Samantha watched him go, a mix of emotions swirling inside her. She'd felt drawn to this kind stranger, but she couldn't understand why. As

Matthew walked away, he couldn't shake the feeling that there was something familiar about the young woman. He chalked it up to the easy rapport they'd shared.

As Matthew and Samantha went their separate ways, neither realized how intertwined their lives already were. They were just strangers who hadn't even told each other their names. Both of them realized later that they hadn't.

Samantha stayed on the bench for a while and then drifted up to the library, figuring it would be a good place to stay out of the storm. As the first drops of rain began to fall, she quickened her steps, making it there just as thunder rolled and lightning flashed.

As Matthew walked away from his conversation with Samantha, the campus showed more signs of life despite, or maybe because of, the approaching storm. A few students hurried along the paths, clutching books and laptops, eager to reach their destinations before the rain hit.

Among the groups of people, one pair caught Matthew's eye. An older man, perhaps in his sixties, was walking with a young boy who looked to be about ten years old. The man had a firm grip on the boy's shoulder, guiding him along. Something about the scene struck Matthew as odd, though he couldn't quite put his finger on why.

The boy had tousled brown hair and wore a red t-shirt that seemed a size too big for him. His face was partially obscured as he kept his head down, but Matthew glimpsed freckles across his nose. There was a nervousness in the boy's steps, a reluctance that contrasted with the purposeful stride of the older man. As they passed by, Matthew overheard a snippet of their conversation.

"Come on," the man said in a low, urgent voice. "We need to hurry."

The boy nodded silently, quickening his pace to keep up with the man's longer strides. Matthew watched them disappear around a corner, a nagging feeling of unease settling in his stomach. He shook his head, trying to dispel the sensation. After all, it was probably just a grandfather taking his grandson for a walk, hurrying to meet someone, perhaps the boy's mother.

A loud clap of thunder, followed by a streak of lightning a few seconds later, told Matthew the storm was almost overhead. Heavy drops of rain fell just as Matthew reached the motel.

Once inside, he drew the curtains and turned on the TV while he popped some popcorn into the room's microwave. Settling down to watch a movie he had purchased early, he couldn't shake the image of the boy and the older man. Something about it didn't seem right, but he wasn't sure what it was. He remembered the missing boy from years before, when he was in Lazy Rivers. But of course, this had nothing to do with that.

Twenty Nine

The next day, Alex did what he did every morning, unless there was an emergency. He went to the diner for coffee and blueberry pancakes. He had once changed that order to a muffin and regretted it. Once he had even gone to a coffee shop to have coffee and some fancy pastry and really regretted that. He liked the diner. He knew everything about it. It had been forbidden territory for his family.

"Too worldly." That's what his dad would say as he slammed his fist onto the dining room table. "This is where we sit and eat. No where else."

Of course, they all knew that wasn't true for his father. For his father, any table in any home, let alone the diner, was where he could eat. Everyone knew his father did whatever he wanted, when he wanted. Alex was sure that his father had been selling whatever was illegal for years. It didn't matter what. And it didn't matter how much money he made, because very little of it made it home to his wife and kids.

The memory of one of his brothers hitting him with a baseball bat could have been any of the times a brother hit him came to mind. They had learned it from their father. He had a sister, but he didn't remember much about her. She had gotten pregnant at sixteen, and she and the boy had left town with the boy's family. From time to time, he thought about trying to find her and decided against it.

He didn't need family. Didn't want it. He enjoyed being alone. There was no one to answer to. *Except the whole town,* he thought to himself. But that was different. He chose to do something for the town. To be responsible, unlike the family he grew up with.

He was glad that everyone in his family either died or left town. Except for his mom. When she died, the only light in the world went out. The only other person in his family that he cared about was his brother, Zach. But that was only because he was the first missing boy. At least, that's what he told himself. And it was because it was a mystery. It wasn't because he wanted his brother back. He barely remembered him anyway.

What troubled him was the idea that it was the beginning of the town's losing boys. Years apart. No particular pattern other than they were all ten. Young to run away. Even so, there was that hope that's what they had done.

The other reason he liked the diner was the bits of conversation that he would pick up. And Betty Jean. She had always treated him with kindness and respect, and he appreciated no one pushed her around. That she could be friendly with Joseph was amazing. Some people said that they were more than friends, and Alex thought that if anyone could be intimate with Joseph, it would be Betty Jean. She was her own woman. He admired her, and when he let himself think about it, loved her. Like his mom.

Today he was hoping to show her a picture. Before leaving yesterday, Serenity had done a quick sketch of the symbol she had seen carved into the tree. He hoped that Betty Jean might know what it meant. When Alex pushed open the diner door, the familiar bell chimed above him, and the scent of coffee and pancakes enveloped him, a comforting constant in his life.

Betty Jean looked up from behind the counter, her weathered face breaking into a warm smile. "Morning, Chief," she called out. "The usual?"

Alex nodded, heading over to his favorite booth where he could see the entire diner. "You know me too well, Betty Jean."

As she poured his coffee, Alex glanced around the diner. There was hardly anyone there, and no sign of Joseph. That wasn't unusual. He was often gone. Betty Jean was the one who kept the diner running.

"Slow morning?" Alex asked as Betty Jean poured his coffee.

"Just the way I like it," she replied with a wink. "Gives me time to catch up on all the town gossip."

Alex smiled and reached into his pocket and pulled out the folded sketch Serenity had given him.

"Have you ever seen this before?" he asked as he unfolded the paper and smoothed it out with his hand.

She leaned over, looked at it, and straightened up, saying nothing. For a moment, Alex thought he saw a flicker of recognition, but it was gone so quickly he couldn't be sure.

"What's this about?"

Alex hesitated, weighing how much to reveal. "Just following up on some leads," he said vaguely. Alex hesitated, then answered, "I thought it might be connected to... well, the missing boys."

At the mention of the missing boys, the few people in the diner stopped talking. Alex knew they were listening, hoping to hear something new. Betty Jean's hand trembled slightly as she picked up the paper to look at it. "Those poor boys," she murmured. "Such a tragedy. I remember when your brother..."

She trailed off, realizing she might have overstepped. Alex stiffened, memories of Zach flooding back. "Yeah," he said gruffly. "It's been a long time."

"You think there's a connection?" Betty Jean whispered. "This has something to do with it?"

Alex shrugged, taking the paper back and putting it into his pocket. "Just exploring all possibilities," he said. "Can't leave any stone unturned."

As Betty Jean set his plate of blueberry pancakes in front of him, Alex couldn't shake the feeling that there was more to her reaction than she let on.

The diner's bell chimed again as new customers entered, breaking the tension. Betty Jean hurried off to greet them, grateful for the chance to walk away. Yes, she had seen that symbol before, but there was no way she was saying anything until she knew more.

Alex turned his attention to his breakfast, but his mind was racing. The symbol, the missing boys, the secrets that seemed to lurk just beneath the surface of this town—it was all connected somehow.

But Serenity had been right. There was no one at the 'haunted house.' There were signs that somebody had been there. But nothing told them where Jimmy might be. And she was right. The symbol was on the tree. It was old, done years before.

How she had known. That was a mystery. Had she actually been to the house and pretended to see it in her memory? He wasn't sure which one he wanted most. That she was for real, or she was an impostor.

As Alex sat there in the diner, surrounded by the familiar sights and sounds of his morning routine, he felt more determined than ever to uncover the truth, no matter where it led him. But even though he tried to fool himself sometimes, he knew he'd never actually find Zach. He was long gone.

Thirty

"Why not come to the nursery?" Tom texted Serenity. "Randy and the crew are on their way there. It will be quieter here."

"Just finishing my walk," she texted back. "I'll be there in thirty."

Serenity pulled into the nursery parking lot, feeling better than the day before. A good night's sleep and the walk had cleared her mind. Just as the storm had cleared the air. Everything was sparkling this morning. She wasn't sure why she had reacted that way about Randy. He was probably a perfectly nice man. Although she was going to ask Tom more about him anyway.

And it was a good idea to meet at the nursery; it was quiet and beautiful, and besides, she expected that her mother would be there too.

Tom and Brad were both waiting for her. Brad was on his way over to her house but had wanted to let her know they'd be doing her studio first. The French doors were on order, but they'd get everything ready for them. Then they'd concentrate on her mother's bedroom.

"It will be a swarm of people in your house for a while," Brad said. "But Randy will be there, overseeing things and using his great eye for detail, to ensure that it goes quickly and that things are done well."

"How well do you know him?" Serenity asked.

"He's only been here for six months or so. But I've worked with him on a few jobs, and he has done excellent work. Plus, all I hear about him are good things. He seems to go out of his way to do things right."

Serenity nodded, thinking that she must be reading something else about him.

"And his dad lived here," Mama said, coming up to the three of them.

"Randy's dad lived in Lazy Rivers?" Tom asked, thinking that was weird. Is that why Randy had come to town? What did that mean?

"Sure, he went to school with us. Moved away about the time Zach went missing. Quiet." Mama said, leaving out the part of how well she had known him. It wasn't important.

"So Randy came here because his dad lived here?" Serenity asked.

"I don't know. I'll ask him," Brad said as he stepped into his truck. "I'll let you know."

"I've got coffee and food in the back," Mama said, and then laughed as Serenity's stomach growled.

Lizzy stood as the three of them arrived, and Serenity was delighted to see how much better she looked.

"You look great, mom. Mama must be taking good care of you."

"Of course I am," Mama said, giving Lizzy a squeeze, helping her sit, and then pouring coffee all around. A pile of pastries sat in the middle of the table.

"Got them from the pastry shop on the way in," Mama said, looking at Serenity's astonished face. Pick what you want; we'll freeze the rest for another day.

For the next thirty minutes, they enjoyed the coffee, pastries, and the morning. The air was fresh and clean from the storm, and as the breeze blew in different directions, swirling around the nursery, they caught the scent of all the flowers and trees.

"Such a beautiful place," Serenity said, breathing in, looking up at the white clouds drifting across the light blue sky. One cloud looked like a bunny, reminding her of Sam, and her breath caught for a moment with the depth of how much she missed her daughter.

Mama nodded. "I've always loved it here. I worked here after high school, which, of course, is how I met your dad, Tom. I'm not sure which one I fell in love with first, the nursery or your dad. Luckily, it was a package deal."

"It was granddad who built this nursery, right?"

"Actually, it was his dad. But it was a small little place then. It was your granddad and dad who turned it into this. But they could because your great-grandfather had been wise enough to buy a lot of acreage back then."

Tom nodded. He knew they owned land far past the nursery, most of it forested, which they maintained and select harvested to keep it healthy. Sometimes they thinned it out and sold the young trees at the nursery.

"The past is what we wanted to talk to you about," Mama said, looking at Tom and Serenity.

Tom and Serenity exchanged looks. Mama looked at Lizzy, and Lizzy nodded at her to continue.

"As you know, we've been friends for a long time. What you may not know is that Lizzy also worked at the nursery after high school. It was really an experiment to see if she could handle being around people and not be bothered by their memories."

Lizzy nodded. "Mom—your grandmother—didn't like it one bit. I knew it was because she was afraid for me. But for a while I loved it. In fact, it was here that I met your dad."

Serenity took a deep breath in. Her mom had never talked about her dad. It scared her a little. Why was she telling her now?

"I'm telling you this because I realize that my mom, and her mom, and all the women before them were wrong. They thought staying away from people would be a good thing. Instead, we were isolated and, at least for me, very lonely."

Seeing her daughter's face, she added, "It's okay. It wasn't your fault. We all made our choices. But now it's time to come out into the world and help you and Samantha learn how to really live."

"So, dad?" Serenity asked.

"Matthew," her mom sighed. Mama reached out and touched her hand and continued the story.

"Matthew was a lovely man. You, of course, got your red hair and blue eyes from him. He was in town on his way somewhere else. He was a journalist." Serenity smiled, thinking that was maybe why Samantha was a writer.

"Anyway, somehow, he ended up at the nursery, saw your mom, and fell in love. At first sight, he told us all. And so he stayed. Your mom got pregnant, and then she did what you Rivers women do and told him to leave. But. It was stupid. I told her. I tell her now. I think she should try to find him. But that's another story. She can tell you more about Matthew later.

"Right now, we have something else to tell you. About another man who came through the nursery at that time."

Lizzy took up the story, her voice barely above a whisper. "An older man came through the nursery one day. It didn't seem important, except there was something... off about him."

"The plants didn't like him," Mama Tate added, her eyes distant with memory. "You know how the plants react to people, Serenity. It was like they were afraid."

Serenity leaned in; her curiosity piqued. "What happened?"

Lizzy and Mama Tate exchanged a look, as if deciding how much to reveal. Finally, Lizzy spoke. "We saw him doing something near the old oak tree at the edge of the property. He was carving something into the trunk."

"A symbol," Mama added. "One we'd never seen before."

Serenity's breath caught in her throat. "Was it like this?" she asked, pulling out a sketch of the symbol she'd seen in her vision.

Both older women gasped. Lizzy's hand trembled as she reached for the paper. "That's it," she whispered. "That's exactly what we saw."

Tom, who had been listening silently, spoke up. "But what does it mean? And why haven't you told anyone about this before?"

Mama shook her head. "We were scared. And then, when the boys started going missing... we thought it might be connected, but we couldn't prove anything."

"And now?" Serenity asked, her heart racing.

Lizzy looked at her daughter, her eyes filled with a mix of fear and determination. "Now, it's time I stopped hiding. And help you find that missing boy."

Thirty One

"Let's go see that oak tree," Lizzy said, after Brad left to check on the house. "We can check it out before too many customers arrive."

"Are you crazy?" Mama asked. "Do you remember how far back that oak tree is? You can't walk there. And I haven't checked on that tree for ages; it might not still be there."

"It's okay," Tom said, glancing at Serenity. "We'll help Lizzy get there. And oak trees live a long time. It's most likely still there."

"But what good will that do?" Mama asked. She felt as if she was the only one paying attention to how weak Lizzy was.

"Memories," Lizzy said, and Serenity nodded.

"Tree memories?" Mama asked.

Serenity laughed. "Well, that sounds like something I would love to see."

Lizzy nodded. "I would too. But no. The memories of the person who carved the symbol. We might pick up one or two."

Mama sighed, realizing that she was outnumbered. "Alright, but we're taking it slow. And if Lizzy gets too tired, we're turning back."

Tom nodded, already moving to help Lizzy up. "I'll grab the golf cart. It'll make the journey easier."

As Tom went to fetch the cart, Serenity helped her mother stand. "Are you sure about this, Mom?" she asked softly.

Lizzy's eyes sparked with determination. "More sure than I've been about anything in a long time."

A few minutes later, they were all settled in the golf cart, Tom at the wheel. He navigated carefully through the nursery, past rows of flowering plants and saplings, towards the wilder, less maintained area at the back of the property.

As they traveled, Mama pointed out changes in the landscape, reminiscing about how things used to be. Lizzy, Tom, and Serenity sat quietly, watching and listening.

Finally, they reached a clearing where an enormous oak tree stood outlined against the blue of the sky. Serenity thought it was the most beautiful tree she had ever seen. It had a presence. It was massive, its branches spreading wide, creating a canopy of green above them.

Tom parked the cart, and they all sat in silence for a moment, taking in the majesty of the ancient tree. Serenity wondered how much history the tree had seen. How many other trees it was a mother to? It gave meaning to the word mother tree. She thought that if it could speak, it would be so wise.

"It's still here," Mama whispered, a mix of awe and trepidation in her voice.

She and Lizzy exchanged looks, remembering how young they had been the last time they were here. Maybe that was why they hadn't said anything. They didn't know what they had seen at the time or what it meant. Actually, Mama thought, all four of us were here then, since she and Lizzy had both been pregnant. How strange that they were here again with their grown babies, Serenity and Tom.

Lizzy's eyes focused on the trunk. "There," she said, pointing to a spot about eye level. "That's where he carved it."

Tom and Serenity helped Lizzy out of the cart and over to the tree. As they got closer, they could see a faint scar in the bark, barely visible after so many years. Lizzy reached out, her fingers trembling as they traced the nearly invisible lines of the old carving. As soon as her skin contacted the bark, she gasped, her eyes going wide.

"Mom?" Serenity said, alarmed. "What is it? What do you see?"

"Oh, this man was so angry. But I don't know why."

Lizzy leaned against the tree, and Tom came up behind her to make sure she would not fall.

"He marked this tree to be a gathering place, mostly men, only a few women. I can't see who they were or what they were saying.

Not all of them were as angry as this man, but they wanted to hear what he had to say."

Serenity closed her eyes, for the first time in her life wanting to see a memory. But instead of seeing something about the tree, she saw Mama's memory of the four of them being together for the first time at the tree. She giggled at the idea of it, surprising herself and everyone else.

"You giggled!" Tom said, still holding onto Lizzy as they turned to look at her. "I don't think I've ever heard you do that before."

"I could blame it on the tree," Serenity said, "but it was because I saw Mama's memory of the four of us here. Those two, pointing at Lizzy and Mama, were hiding in the brush back there watching him carve the symbol."

"But we weren't born yet," Tom said, and then, registering what she meant, started laughing. Soon all four were laughing, and if they had looked up, they would have seen the leaves of the tree waving above them, as if it were laughing with them.

As they helped Lizzy back to the golf cart, Mama said, "For some reason, I think this wasn't about something bad happening. I think they were trying to do something good together."

"It's possible," Lizzy answered. "He was angry about something, but it doesn't mean that he was an evil person. It could mean the exact opposite."

"And maybe the plants pulled back from him only because of his anger," Tom added.

"But does this have anything to do with the missing boys?" Serenity asked. "Because Jimmy is still missing and we know nothing other than this symbol is here, and on the tree at the old house where I saw Jimmy. I looked it up on the internet and couldn't find anything that looked like it. So it's possible it is something that man made up and only pertains to something around here."

"True," Tom said. "And if that's true, there are probably other people in town who know what that symbol means."

By the time they got back to the nursery, it was busy, and Mama and Tom headed off to help with customers. Brad had returned and caught Serenity up on what was going on at her house. It sounded so chaotic she decided to stay at the nursery too and help out, but first she took her mother back to her room at Mama's house.

Mama had put a lovely soft lounge chair in the room for her, and Serenity helped her into it. There were books on the side table and a thermos of water. Seeing Serenity take in the surroundings, Lizzy said, "Yes, I am well taken care of here." Lifting a tin box by her chair, she opened it to show her it was full of snacks and energy bars. "This is to make sure I keep eating!"

As Serenity tucked in the blanket around her, Lizzy added, "I want to find those boys. It's the most important thing we can do."

"I agree, mom. We will. One way or another, we will find them."

Neither of them mentioned it was possible that Jimmy was already dead. And the boys before him. But that didn't mean they couldn't find them and bring them home.

And Serenity didn't tell her she had seen another man hiding with Lizzy and Mama, watching the man carve the symbol. She kept waiting for one of them to mention him, but they never did. And that worried her more than anything. What more were the two of them hiding?

Thirty Two

Randy took one more walk through the house, making sure everyone was on track and didn't need anything, before slipping into the front seat of his truck. He wasn't going anywhere; he just needed to call his dad. The idea had been nagging at him for a few days, and he just didn't think he could wait one more day to make his regular Saturday afternoon call. But what would his dad think of him calling him early? He might worry.

That's what he had been telling himself for the last few days, but finally he couldn't take it anymore. He was the one who set the timing of the calls, not his dad. Maybe his dad would like to be called more often. That idea almost brought tears to his eyes. He had been so busy trying to find himself that he hadn't thought about how his dad must feel, all alone in the house.

The phone rang for more than the usual few rings, but then his dad wasn't expecting the call. When he did answer, he was worried, just as Randy had feared.

"What's wrong?"

"Nothing, Dad. I was just at a job and thought about you and decided to call."

There was a long pause, and Randy held his breath. "What kind of job?" John Carver asked his son.

"A big old house. I'm also overseeing the day-to-day stuff. So much needs to be done. And Dad, we—I—could use you here."

Another long pause. Randy thought he heard his dad sniff. Was he crying?

"Dad?"

"Where's here?"

"Not far," Randy said, mad at himself even more than he had been for neglecting his dad. He hadn't even told him about the town he'd moved to this time, and it had been a good six months.

"Lazy Rivers," he said.

Another long pause. This time he was sure his dad was crying because he heard him put the phone down and walk away.

"Dad!" Randy yelled on the phone. "Dad, come back to the phone, or I'm getting in my truck and coming there right now."

He heard the phone being picked up and another pause before his dad cleared his throat and said, "Yeah, I know that town."

"So will you come?"

John Carver looked down at his bare arm, saw the faded scar, swallowed, and said, "Sure," doing his best to keep any emotions out of his voice.

"Great, you can stay with me. When can you get here?"

John looked around the living room, the mess he lived in because he didn't care anymore, and realized that he had reached a turning point. If he went there, nothing would be the same. He would be forced to care.

"I can be there tomorrow afternoon."

Randy gave him his address and hung up, thinking now he'd done it. His dad was coming. It would either be the best thing he had done or the worst. Either way, he had made a decision to help. It was what he did. It surprised him how long it had taken to decide to help the one person who probably needed him the most.

John Carver thought about his life. It had been a good one. But since his wife died, he had stopped caring. Now that he was thinking about returning to Lazy Rivers, he realized it was as if time had paused and he was living in a kind of limbo. As he stood in the middle of his cluttered living room, phone still in hand, he felt his heart beating, racing, and afraid. Lazy Rivers. The name alone brought back a flood of memories he'd spent decades trying to forget.

He shuffled to the bathroom and splashed cold water on his face. In the mirror, he barely recognized the man staring back at him. When had he gotten so old? So lost? Moving to the closet, he reached behind all the shoes thrown around the floor of the closet and pulled out an old shoe box. He knew what was inside. A collection of newspaper clippings.

Opening the lid, they lay there, yellowed with age, staring up at him. All the headlines about a missing boy in Lazy Rivers. John's fingers traced the faded scar on his arm. He remembered the night he got it—the night everything changed. The symbol, the oak tree, the sadness that had followed him ever since.

After speaking to his dad, Randy returned to the house renovation. As he supervised the work, his mind wandered to his father's reaction. Why had the mention of Lazy Rivers affected him so strongly? What secrets was he hiding? They had been so close. How had they drifted apart?

As the day progressed, Randy was caught up in all the questions and problems that needed to be solved with the house, but when he stood still, he could feel the questions swirling around him like a tornado, getting ready to sweep away the life he knew.

Brad had come and gone after walking through the house with Randy to make sure they were all on the same page. That's when

Randy learned his dad went to school with Elizabeth Rivers and Mama Tate.

"You didn't know?" Brad had asked.

"Clueless. Did you know?"

"Just learned it today," Brad answered. They were standing outside, looking at the mess of a backyard, holding cups of coffee.

"Wonder what it means," Randy said, and added, "Have you ever seen Serenity's daughter? There aren't any pictures of anyone in the house. Isn't that kind of weird?"

"I suppose. Mama has her family pictures all over her house. Different people. And no, I haven't. She hasn't been back here for years. I'm sure she's beautiful, though. Why?"

"No reason. Curious. My dad is coming to Lazy Rivers. I'm going to add him to the crew, if you don't mind. He taught me everything I know, so he will help this go faster."

Brad clapped him on his back and told him that was a great idea. He'd let Lizzy and Mama know his dad was coming back to town. They'd probably be thrilled to see him.

Or not, Randy thought to himself.

By late afternoon, Serenity arrived at the house, looking exhausted. She said she'd stay out of their way, but she needed to be home. Randy was ready to call it quits for the day. Before heading upstairs to her bedroom, Serenity turned to Randy and looked at him. They had intentionally saved her room for last so she could have a place to be while the rest of the house was torn apart.

"Thanks for doing this," she said. And then, when he just stared back, she asked if everything was okay.

He thought about telling her about the eyes in the mirror and about his dad, but decided against it. On the other hand, he worried if she would see a memory that he didn't want her to see, which included both those moments.

He nodded, forcing a smile. "Just fine, ma'am. We're making good progress."

"Serenity, please," she said, and waited. It felt as if he wanted to ask her something.

"Yes, ma'am, I mean, Serenity."

As she headed upstairs, Randy couldn't shake the feeling that he was standing on the edge of something big, something that connected him, his father, the Rivers women, and the missing boys of Lazy Rivers. That night, as Randy prepared for his father's arrival the next day, he found himself unable to sleep. He paced his small house, mind racing with questions.

What would his father reveal when he arrived? Had he ever really known his father? And more importantly, was Randy ready for what he had to say?

Thirty Three

After his breakfast at the diner, Alex spent the entire day trying to piece together what was the same and what was different about the boys that had gone missing. However, to get to that point, the first thing he had done—he was amazed it hadn't been done before, but the past sheriff had been useless anyway—was to put together a list of boys who were actually missing. Because rumors were one thing, but facts were another.

The town gossip reminded him of the game "whisper down the alley." Was any of it true in the end, or simply a distortion of what really happened? What he wanted to know was if a boy went missing, did he return later? Or did he let people know where he was if he didn't come home? Did anyone document that? It turned out that they hadn't, at least not very well.

After searching through old files for most of the morning, he discovered that there were eight boys still unaccounted for. Next, he and his assistant checked with the remaining members of the families of the ones reported missing to find out if they still were. In the end, there were four left. A much smaller number than talked about, but four was still four too many.

By late afternoon, he was ready to study the four missing boys' files. What was similar about them? The biggest problem he could see was that the four missing boys were taken so many years apart, so he didn't see how it could be the same person talking to them. If that was what really happened. His brother's kidnapping was fifty years ago, The next boy was thirty years ago, and then ten years ago, and now Jimmy was only a few days ago.

He started with his brother, Zach. He didn't want to. It was hard to be dispassionate about it. After all, he knew his family better than any other family, even if he hadn't really known his brother. The little he remembered—he wasn't sure if it was his memory or what he'd been told. It occurred to him that Serenity could be very helpful. But he wondered if she saw the memory as it happened or the memory that was altered every time it was brought to thought.

That was the thing about memories. They ended up always being false. And some of them were false from the outset. Which led him down a rabbit hole of wondering what use memories were anyway, since they were simply stories that kept getting rewritten. *But*, he thought, *if we didn't have some memories, then we wouldn't have a past.* And that felt as if he'd be untethered in the world.

Who were you without your memories? But if you rewrote them all the time, what use were they?

Finally, he dragged himself back from the questions about memories, opened each file of the four remaining boys, and started a list on the whiteboard in his office. Here's what he knew.

Zach Williams was 10. His father was mean. In fact, in Alex's eyes, the whole family was mean. Zach went to school and didn't come home.

Michael Anderson was 10. He disappeared on his way home from baseball practice. There was very little information about home life.

Danny Foster was 10. He was last seen riding his bike near the town park. His parents divorced shortly before his disappearance.

Jimmy Hunter was/is 10. He had an angry father. He had been playing in the backyard and had gone to the old house.

The only thing that tied them together that he could see was they were all ten years old. That's it. There were so few notes on the other two boys that he knew nothing about their home life. None of the boys looked like each other, at least as far as he could tell. Jimmy didn't look like his brother Zach, anyway. Jimmy was/is a lanky ten-year-old with a mop of unruly brown hair and freckles and hazel eyes with a gap-toothed grin.

His brother Zach had spiky blond hair, was short for his age, and had brown eyes. If he were alive now, he didn't know what he would look like. But that was daydreaming. He knew his brother had died somewhere, but how and who did it?

All he really knew about Michael and Danny was that they were ten when they went missing. Which meant that all he knew for certain was that over fifty years, four boys were missing. Did they really have a missing boy problem? Or had it become a story that the town told? Not that it changed the importance of the missing boys, but it changed the tone of the story. How could one person be responsible for all this for all these years? And if they were, why? Why these boys? And what had been done with them?

Alex thought all the answers for all the boys lay with finding Jimmy. Still, there were people in town who'd been around since the first boy went missing. What did they remember? Maybe they hadn't told the whole story. Even as implausible as it may seem, they could be responsible. Or at least there was more that they had never told.

People like Joseph, Pete, and even Betty Jean. How well did he know any of them, anyway?

And then there was the symbol carved into the tree. Tom had called him earlier that day and told him about the tree at the nursery with the same symbol and the brief memory that Serenity had about it. Alex thought it was interesting that Serenity was her name, because for him, he felt anything but serene when he thought about her. Maybe her name was wishful thinking on the part of her mother.

All his life he had been afraid of the Rivers women—not that he told anyone, but he had been. He didn't want them "seeing" what was going on in his family. It was why he kept his distance. He had no desire or need to be pitied. But now that he had spent some time with Serenity, he realized she wouldn't feel pity. What she would feel he didn't know, but it wouldn't be pity.

As he closed the files and prepared to go home, Alex decided to ask for more help from Serenity in the morning. His feelings for her, not that he was sure what he felt, would have to be put aside. The most important thing to do was find Jimmy, and in doing so, perhaps solve the mysteries of the other three boys. And always, in the back of his mind, perhaps find out what happened to his brother.

What if Zach wasn't dead and was still out there somewhere? But if so, why hadn't he come home? To Alex, that meant Zach had to be dead, and it was his job to find out what happened. He'd bring him home somehow, along with Jimmy. That was a promise he intended to keep, but in his heart, he knew it might not be possible. Still, he could hope, and if he stopped hoping, he might as well just give up. And that was something he was not willing to do.

Thirty Four

W as any part of his life not filled with junk? His house. His mind. Junk. *How had this happened?* John Carver asked himself. How had everything gone this way? He had practically disappeared from himself since his wife Mary died. *Is this what she would have wanted for him?* He knew the answer. She'd be furious over what he had done to himself, or not done to himself.

Not that he hadn't always had the secret buried inside him about why he had left Lazy Rivers. But while she was alive, it had stayed hidden, even from himself most of the time. Then he had more important things to think about, like building a life for their family.

And it had been a very good life. The best part had been sharing time with his son while they worked on jobs together. Then, after Mary died, Randy left, taking with him any chance of his being happy again. John would never tell him, but he had lived from

Saturday to Saturday for his son's calls. But now Randy asked him to do something that seemed impossible. Return to Lazy Rivers. And he had agreed. What had he been thinking?

So for the last hour he had stared at the battered, empty suitcase that lay open on the bed. It was waiting for him to put his big boy pants on and get moving. Instead, he was frozen in place, wondering how many years it had been since he had pulled the sheets tight and smoothed out the quilt his wife made of memories.

There was a patch made from Randy's first outfit, his wife's favorite dress, the shirt he was wearing when they met. It was their life spread out before him. The life he had with Mary. She was the one who made order out of chaos. He made the mess. But this mess, the one waiting for him to fix, she hadn't known about, and even if she had, she couldn't have done anything about it.

This was the one he had tried to forget, and if his Randy hadn't called, he could have continued on pretending it never happened. But it had, and now he had a chance to fix it. If that were possible. That remained to be seen. But he'd never find out, just staring at the suitcase.

Put stuff in and go, he said to himself. *Stop being a coward.* Running his hand one more time over the quilt that he hoped he'd see again, he rummaged through his closet and drawers, threw the mess in—why be orderly now—and snapped the case shut.

Then, catching a glimpse of the box with the newspaper clippings, he tucked it under his arm. It might be useful when he tried to explain what had happened. For a moment, he stared at the picture of his wife and son that stood on the table by the bed, the last thing he saw each night and the first thing he saw in the morning.

No, he wouldn't take the photo. He'd come back to it once he had cleaned up the mess he had left in Lazy Rivers. His truck was gassed up, ready to go. Filled with junk. Throwing the suitcase in, stuffing the shoebox under the back seat, he put the truck in reverse, said goodbye to the last fifty years of his life, and headed back to where he had run from.

It was time to go home.

In Lazy Rivers, Randy was busy cleaning his own house. His dad was coming. Not that his house was messy, but he wanted it to be perfect for his dad. It wasn't really his house. It was a rental, thinking he would never stay long enough anywhere to want to buy something. Until now. But he cleaned it anyway as if it were his own, putting away some things he left out since he was the only one who saw it.

As he put stuff away, he pretended he was his mother, who wanted everything to be in order. *What would mom do with this?*

Randy asked himself as he cleaned. An orderly house would be what his dad would expect since they had always lived in her orderly home together. This would be the first time anyone other than himself and his landlord had been in his house since he moved in.

Not that he didn't have friends. He loved meeting people, but he liked keeping them separate from his house. He needed the time after work to collect himself. But now, for the first time in over ten years, he'd be sharing his house with someone else. Yes, it was his dad. And he'd lived and worked with him for years before he left to travel. But this was different. His dad was different. After his mom died, his dad lost interest in so many things that they loved to do together.

Saturday afternoon calls had kept them in touch, but not close. Now instead of a call, his dad would be standing at his door, live-and-in-person. Since his dad insisted on just a phone call, he hadn't actually seen him after all this time. A part of him was worried about what his dad would look like. He should have gone home to check on him.

After straightening everything that he could in his house, Randy headed to the job site, hoping Serenity would still be there. He had some questions to ask her about her studio. He had given his dad the address of the house and said he'd meet him there to show him around. His dad had barely answered, saying he knew the place.

Randy thought working on a project together first might help break the tension between them. They had spent many hours together building things. In fact, of all the people he had worked with through the years, his dad was the easiest person to work with. Somehow, they both knew what to do next without speaking. The Rivers house needed his dad. *And so do I,* Randy realized.

Serenity was waiting for him, standing in the yard with a cup of something in her hands.

"I thought you might have questions for me," she said. "Alex called and wanted to talk, but I told him I thought you would need to talk to me before I leave."

"I did, I do…," Randy stuttered, trying to get himself to say her name. He didn't know why he was so nervous around her. He didn't need to win her approval, and yet when he thought about it, that was exactly what he wanted. But why? She was just another client. What he couldn't figure out was why every time he was with her, he thought about the eyes in his rear-view mirror.

A few minutes later, they had cleared up some questions he had about what she wanted in her studio. As she started to leave, for some reason, he blurted out that his dad was coming to town to help with the house.

"Your dad? I think he grew up with my mom and Mama Tate."

"Yes. I just learned that he grew up here. For some reason, he had never mentioned it to me."

"Maybe he didn't think it mattered," Serenity said, but even as she said it, she knew that wasn't true. "I'll let Mama and Lizzy know he's coming. I'm sure they will want to get together."

Randy nodded, went to his truck to get his tool bag, and wondered once again why his dad had never mentioned that he had grown up in Lazy Rivers. His dad had kept where he grew up a secret. Why was that? Randy prayed it had nothing to do with the missing boys, but he was afraid that it did.

Thirty Five

Serenity met Alex at the diner. It was his suggestion. And as much as she wanted to say no, she also knew she had to get over her phobia of being around people. Before leaving the house, she had called Mama to check on her mother and heard she had a good night's sleep and that all was well.

"I'll be there later," she said. "And by the way, Randy's dad is coming to town."

There was a brief pause before Mama said, "Okay," and hung up. Serenity wondered what that was all about, but put the question aside until she could ask her face-to-face.

As she drove to the diner, she thought about Randy and his happiness about his father coming to visit. *It must be nice*, she thought. *You call, and they come. She called Samantha, but had she come?* Serenity knew it was not fair to be snarky about Randy's dad coming just because she couldn't get her own daughter to come home. But still. She was upset. As her eyes welled up, she willed the emotion of sadness and even anger to stop.

She knew people thought she felt nothing, that she was too matter-of-fact. But the truth was, she felt everything. She just kept it to herself. And seeing Alex was part of the problem. He wasn't just some boy she used to see at school. She had liked him. But he was distant, and so was she. Besides, that was so long ago, it didn't matter anymore. And yet, it felt as if it did, and she didn't like that at all.

Determined not to give any of herself away, she steeled herself against the onslaught of memories that wanted recognition. She paused at the door of the diner before opening it, shutting everything out but the present, and stepped in. As she opened the door, the smell of coffee and food enveloped her, and she lost a little of her fear of being with people. For a moment, she let go of the reason she had come there and let herself be enveloped by the smell and feel of the diner.

Then Betty Jean looked up and pointed to the back of the diner, giving her a friendly smile. But there was a worry behind it, and Serenity hoped that Betty Jean was okay. She couldn't imagine Lazy Rivers without Betty Jean's presence. Betty Jean knew everyone and everything. Which, Serenity reminded herself, meant she also knew more than she was saying about the missing boys. And since she knew everything, of course, she knew she was here to meet with Alex.

And of course he would wait for her, sitting with his back against the wall. She had seen him do that as a kid, always afraid of people sneaking up on him. What she hadn't told him when she told him about the memory she saw is that she also saw what his dad used to do. If she had that history, she'd sit that way, too. It was an ingrained habit, just like her pausing before entering a building with people in it. Protection. They both had that in common.

What she didn't like, but knew she'd have to do, was tell him she saw that memory about his father, given that his brother was the first boy to go missing. It was entirely possible that he had run away from an abusive dad who got a kick out of coming up from behind his kids and pushing them down, or slapping them so hard on the head that they fell down.

And it was entirely possible that the Hunter boy had done the same thing, given that she had also seen a memory of anger directed against Jimmy by his dad. Were all the boys abused? When Alex called, he mentioned he had researched the missing boys, and that there were only four missing, not the many that the town constantly referred to. Maybe they enjoyed calling their town "the place where boys go missing."

Not that four wasn't four too many, but she couldn't see how it was one person doing all the taking. Fifty years was a long time to be taking boys. Unless the person was young when it started, and Lazy Rivers was not the only place he took boys from. That was always a possibility.

Alex stood as she approached the table and actually gave her a little smile. She wondered if he knew he smiled. But she smiled back and watched as his smile grew big enough that the skin around his eyes crinkled. When the unwanted thought of how handsome he was when he smiled came to her, she was glad that there was no one there who could read thoughts like she saw memories.

But it surprised her how happy she was to be there. They were trying to solve a terrible puzzle together, and they should both be very solemn about it. Instead, she felt a tiny sliver of happiness worming its way through her system, and she wondered if the smell of pancakes and coffee would always remind her of this moment.

Within seconds after sitting down, Betty Jean was pouring coffee, and everything returned to normal. If finding missing boys was normal. As unreasonable as it sounded, Serenity was glad that there was something that important to keep her distracted from her long-buried feelings for Alex Williams. However, if she could see thoughts instead of memories, she would have known that Alex was having the same problem.

It's totally inappropriate, Alex told himself, forcing himself to look away from Serenity and instead smile up at Betty Jean, who winked at him the same way Joseph had winked at him. *Oh, God, he thought they know.* Keeping his face down, he waited for the blush to recede, wondering how. *How did she know?*

Joseph stood in the doorway watching Alex and Serenity and wondering when they would figure it out. Alex and Serenity. They had always been an item. They just had never noticed. But once they did, what else would they notice? Something more dangerous to him and the others?

Betty Jean had told him they had found the symbol on the oak tree at the nursery and the haunted house. Unconsciously, he checked his left arm to make sure his sleeve was rolled down. It had been stupid to put it there. But they had made a pact, and it was a reminder of what they had done, and would do together. None of them fully realizing then what they had agreed to, and its consequences.

Thirty Six

Tom watched his mother after she hung up the phone and worried about how pale she had become. But when she turned to look at him, she smiled as if nothing was wrong and asked if he had a good night's sleep and did he need anything?

"Yes, and nope, I'm good."

"I'm going to check on Lizzy," she said and patted his arm as she walked past.

Tom shrugged. Something didn't feel right, but he supposed it was just his mom being worried about Lizzy. He was worried about her too, even though she had seemed to get better every day. But in general, he felt worried. It wasn't just the missing boy. It was as if there was a fog of worry that had settled over him and followed him around. He felt like the cartoon Pig Pen, who always had a cloud of dust over his head.

Brad had asked about it, but he had shrugged and said he didn't know what was wrong. Something just didn't feel right, but he'd be okay. And that's what he told himself now, too. His assurance hadn't worked on Brad, and he wasn't sure it was working on him either. He could hear the murmur of voices in the office where he knew his mother had settled Lizzy for the morning. She said she wasn't going to leave her home alone in her house, and besides it was good for Lizzy to get out and do something.

He had no idea what she was having her do in the office, but it did need some tidying up. Maybe he could get her to help him a little today in the potting shed. Planting seeds and potting plants always made him feel better, and he thought it would do the same for her. It would also keep her away from the customers and their memories, which he knew was a problem for her. For all the Rivers women. Which made him think of Samantha. If he had her phone number, he would call her and see if he could shame her into coming home.

Tom remembered Sam as a kid when she came with her mother to visit. She was curious and happy, but maybe she had withdrawn more as she headed into her teen years. But he knew calling her was a bad idea and was glad he didn't have the number so he wouldn't make that mistake. She would come back when it was the right time. Besides, his mother's magic—really just attention and unconditional love—was working for Lizzy. *And Serenity being around*, he added to himself. He was better too since she came home. His current worry would be much worse if he was alone with it.

He moved closer to the office, trying to hear what they were talking about. He heard the words, "He's coming back," and then his mother's voice loud and clear, "Stop sneaking around out there, and just come in."

Rolling his eyes, not at his mother but at himself, thinking he could put anything over on her, he opened the door to find the two of them sitting at the office table drinking coffee and eating donuts.

There was an extra setting. "For me?"

They both laughed. "We wondered how long it would be before you would try to listen."

"Not very long," his mother laughed. "Your coffee is still hot."

"Okay, you caught me. Who's coming back?"

"The other person who was there that day."

"The day you saw the man at the oak tree?"

Lizzy nodded. "Yes. Randy's dad, John Carver."

"Start at the beginning," Tom said.

Mama sighed, looked at Lizzy, who nodded at her to go ahead, and said, "That was Serenity on the phone. When she saw Randy at the house, he told her that he had asked his dad to come visit and help with the construction."

"And?"

"And, remember we told you that we grew up with Randy's dad? Well, sometimes he helped out at the nursery. And the day we followed that man to the nursery, he was with us. It's not a big deal, except he left town right after Alex's brother went missing. He has never come back until now," Mama said.

"Actually, I thought that was why Randy moved here, but when he was here one day, I asked him why he picked Lazy Rivers, and he said it was just a town on the map. At the time, I didn't realize he was John Carver's son."

"So you think Carver senior leaving town had something to do with Zach going missing?"

"Perhaps. Or maybe he knew more about that man at the tree. Or it was just a coincidence," Mama said, and Lizzy nodded in agreement.

Tom looked at the two of them, thinking they were leaving something out, and wondered what it was, but then his phone dinged. Glancing down, he saw it—a text from Serenity with a line drawing she had done of the symbol they had seen on the tree. She had cleaned it up so it was easier to see what it was.

"I think this looks like a flame, don't you?" She asked.

"Yes," Tom texted back. "But fire has so many meanings. So what did this mean?"

"Exactly," Serenity said. "Ask Mama and Lizzy what they think."

After putting a thumbs up on her text, Tom showed the picture to his mom and Lizzy.

"That helps to see it like that. I remember how clear it was back then," Lizzy said. "We thought of it as something scary, like the devil's flame, but now I wonder if it meant that. Flames can also be a guide, or warmth."

"And I've seen this design before," Tom said. "I just can't think of where. No, I don't mean the one at the house that Serenity saw. On a person. Like a tattoo. But who? And where?"

Lizzy leaned back in her chair and closed her eyes. This time she was welcoming a memory. Tom's. If she could see what he remembered, it might help. As long as he hadn't altered the memory in the meantime, it could point them in the right direction to find Jimmy Hunter.

Thirty Seven

Mama gave Lizzy some old files to sort out, scan, and put into the computer to keep her busy, checked on the store, and sent Tom out to the potting shed. She knew that would help him sort through his own thoughts. Once that was done, and she was sure no one would need her for the next hour or two, she headed out into the edge of the nursery. She wanted to see the tree again. There were things she had to figure out.

She knew Tom was feeling worried. She thought he was probably worried about her, even though he didn't know why. He'd always been that way, picking up her feelings. And yes, she was worried. It was stupid, really. Just because John Carver was returning to town shouldn't cause worry. And just because he had been there that day when the man carved the symbol on the tree shouldn't cause worry. But she was worried anyway.

Are you sure that's what you are feeling? she asked herself. *Or is it anticipation, not knowing what will happen when you see him?* "Bah, feelings," she said as she walked, her hiking boots kicking up dust. It had been so dry lately. It either didn't rain or it poured rain. So unlike the summers she knew as a child. Not this constant cycle of dry and then so much rain it caused floods.

Everything was different. Not just the weather. Her. She was old. The trouble was she didn't want to be old, and she didn't feel old most of the time. If she didn't look in the mirror, most of the time she thought she was still young. She remembered her dad keeping his birthday at thirty-nine forever. "Like Jack Benny," he used to say.

But the mirror told a different story. The mirror reflected back to her all of her seventy years and some. Wrinkles, gray hair, and more weight than she used to have showed up in the mirror. And then that made her feel as if time was passing, and there wasn't much time left until she'd be gone. And the worry over being old had increased when she had thought her best friend was going to die. Now she wasn't so sure that was going to happen, and it eased her fear a little. If Lizzy could hang around with her for at least another twenty years, they could pretend together that they were still young. Who knows what could happen then?

As she walked, unconsciously checking on plants as she passed them, her finger tips brushing the close ones, she thought about telling Lizzy one of her secrets. It was one that wouldn't hurt to tell. It was about what her husband, Ted, had left as a legacy for the town. She'd kept it a secret because he had asked her to. But she thought now that Ted wouldn't mind if she told Lizzy, and it was time to tell Tom too.

Her husband, a good man from the beginning, had left a trust for the town that was to be used to maintain it. More specifically, he wanted it to remain beautiful and get more beautiful over time. He had been very detailed about what the money could be used for and what it couldn't. And once a year, an auditor made sure that was what was happening with the money.

Ted Tate had been following the wishes of his father, who had loved Lazy Rivers. Ted's father was aware that for a small town, keeping up with its needs could be hard. So he made it possible. While he was alive, he funded projects that kept the town well maintained, plus he donated money towards the planting of trees and gardens. It was because of his father that the town had become more and more beautiful, and Ted wanted to continue that.

Mama was proud to be part of that legacy, although she did nothing other than supply plants when they needed them. "Always give them the best," her husband had whispered to her before he died. And she had. She missed him now just as much as she had when he died over twenty years ago. And there were times she was lonely, even though she would never admit that.

There was no one else for me but Ted Tate, she thought as she walked. And then she snorted. "Right. Tell the truth to yourself, girlfriend," she said out loud since there was no one to hear her. "You know there was someone before him. But it hadn't worked out then, and it wouldn't work out now," she said, still talking out loud. The trees already knew this story. "Besides, I don't want it to. I have Lizzy, Tom, and Brad and the nursery to look out for."

By the time she was almost to the tree, Mama had managed to talk herself out of the funk she had started to fall into. Life was good, and it would get even better once they found Jimmy. Brushing away the last branch before stepping into the clearing, she stopped short. There was someone else at the tree. Still long and lean, maybe too lean. His back was to her as he traced the symbol on the tree. But she knew who he was.

John Carver had come back.

Thirty Eight

Samantha was trying to decide if she should call first or just show up. Either way was going to be painful. What she really wanted to do was stay in the motel forever or go home. But neither of them was something she could do. She had promised her grandmother she'd come see her, and of course she wanted to. Even though she didn't.

Mixed feelings were not Sam's favorite thing, even though she often had them. It bugged her that people like her mother seemed to always know who they were and what they wanted. She was wise enough to know that probably wasn't the truth. It just felt that way. But she did know her mother was straight-forward. Get the job done that needed to be done with as few outward feelings as possible.

Sometimes it had felt as if Serenity wanted her daughter to be like she was. And because of that, they had often clashed. She wondered if her mother and Lizzy had clashed and thought that was probably true, but not in the same way. If she was going to be honest with herself, she knew that she didn't really know either of them. Not that she knew many people, or anybody if it came right down to it, but she really didn't know the two women in her life that were part of a long line of women.

The Rivers women. That's how they were known, as if they were a separate identity from the rest of the world. Which in some way they were. And she was part of that, like it or not. *Which means I've got to get there today*, Sam thought to herself. She still didn't know if she was going to call first, but to make sure she would leave, after getting her writing done for the day, she checked out of her room.

With everything in her car, she still didn't want to go. Delaying the inevitable, she decided to stop at one of the coffee shops she had seen on Main Street. After parking, she thought about visiting the art gallery but decided against it. That was her mother's thing. She was going to stay out of it, just like she liked her mother staying out of her life.

She'd tell her about it when she saw her—something to break the ice. Of course that would mean she'd have to tell her that she had been in Spring Falls for a few days. Would she understand? She didn't know, proving once again that she didn't know either her mother or grandmother very well. And she should. After all, who else did she know that shared the annoying gift of seeing memories?

As she stepped out of the car, she was reminded of her annoying gift as a boy brushed past her as he stepped onto his skateboard. It was a brief memory of hugging a woman who could have been his mother, but she was gone now. And it was his missing part of the memory that was clear. She looked at the boy as he passed. Nothing about him showed grief; if anything, he seemed angry. That was one thing seeing memories had taught her. What people showed on the surface was rarely what was going on inside.

Like me, she thought. I probably look like I know what I'm doing, but I don't. She thought of the many days of sadness that sometimes seem to take over, for apparently no good reason. But did she tell anyone? Of course not. First of all, who would she tell, and then what good would it do? It was only on those days that she missed not having a friend to talk to. Otherwise, she loved being her own person, doing her own thing, in her own way. *Sure,* she told herself. *That's enough for you.*

She ordered a coffee, trying the house specialty, a special blend of flavors, and settled into a table in the back. The warm, rich notes of the coffee, which surprisingly did have a hint of blueberry as promised, gave her an idea for her story. Opening her computer, she thought she'd get some more writing done before heading to Lazy Rivers.

"Do you want to be distracted?" She heard a man say, and looked up to see the same man she had seen in the motel lobby and then on campus.

"I think that would be a good thing," she answered, closing the computer and gesturing for him to sit down. "I've done enough writing for today."

But before closing the computer, she added a note to herself about the idea she just had. She knew if it didn't get written down, she probably wouldn't remember it.

Matthew moved a chair over to the table as he said, "So wait, you're a writer? You let me go on about being a journalist and didn't mention you write?"

Sam sighed, thinking that she had a choice to make. Actually meet this nice man and have an honest conversation, or do what she normally did. Hide. He sat across from her, a kind-looking man who was probably someone's favorite grandfather, and decided to see if she could be normal for a minute. She prayed she wouldn't see any memories while she talked to him.

"Sorry, I tend to be private. But we keep running into each other, so perhaps the universe wants us to meet. Yes, I write books."

Matthew looked at the woman sitting across from him and decided to tell her that he thought she looked familiar.

"I agree we should formally meet. But are you sure we haven't met before? You seem so familiar to me, but I can't place when that would be. Maybe I've seen your picture on a book jacket? But then I think I would remember. After all, you'd be a hard person to forget, since you are quite beautiful."

Sam's eyes filled with tears, surprising her. What was that about? Just because he was kind and gave her a compliment.

"Are you okay?" Matthew asked.

"Yes," Sam said, wondering why the tears—maybe they were happy tears. "Perhaps we should start with our names, and maybe that's how you will figure out if you've seen me before."

Matthew laughed. "That is so wise. Of course we should. My name, young lady, is Matthew Nelson. I'm a journalist who loves to tell stories about people all over the world."

"Nice to meet you," Sam said, sticking out her hand to shake his. "Forgetting to use her fake last name, she said, I'm Samantha Rivers. I'm a writer. I love to tell stories that pop into my head."

Matthew missed everything she said after she said the name Rivers. It couldn't be, but now that he thought about it, it was obvious. She was a Rivers woman. And there was only one person she could be. She was Elizabeth Rivers' granddaughter.

Taking her hand, this time it was his eyes that filled with tears. "I see it now. You are Lizzy's granddaughter."

For the first time in Sam's life, she understood what it meant to have a time stop. Nothing moved. The world stood still. There were no sounds, no smells, nothing. It was as if she had pushed pause on a television show.

And then the pause was over, and everything about her life felt different.

Thirty Nine

"Where are you heading to, Serenity?" Alex asked as they stood outside the diner under one of the many trees that grew along the roads of Lazy Rivers. Until Serenity moved away, she hadn't really noticed how many trees their town had compared to other places. And small pocket gardens instead of empty lots. She had appreciated Lazy Rivers before; now she was beginning to wonder why she had left.

Of course she knew. Too many people were always staring at her and her mother. But now she realized it didn't matter. Or not as much as it had. A gentle breeze carried the scent of the mountain laurel bush planted nearby. It was a stark contrast to the heavy atmosphere surrounding their conversation in the diner. They had discussed the case and realized they were no further along than before. No real suspects. No real clues. A symbol that meant something to somebody, but they still didn't know what or who.

"Had they ever had a suspect?" Serenity had asked Alex as he reviewed the cases with her. The truth was they had not. And neither did he. He was beginning to feel as ineffectual as the police chief before him. At least he had interviewed everyone who knew Jimmy, not like when his brother disappeared and the sheriff had written him off as a runaway within days, barely talking to anyone. No one had cared enough, not even his own family.

Serenity had asked him more about his brother than anyone had bothered to ask him before. She admitted that she saw his memory of the abuse his dad had inflicted on all of them, and based on that, perhaps it was true that he had run away.

"Or my dad did something to him," he had mumbled, looking down at his coffee.

Serenity had not said anything. Instead, she waited for him to look up at her before she asked if he really thought that was what had happened.

"No. He was mean and cruel, but I don't think he could have killed him. On the other hand, that would make more sense than four boys missing over a fifty-year time frame. And no specific timing to it either. It could be four different reasons why they are missing, and one of them could be because dad killed Zach."

Serenity had nodded at what he said, adding that it was possible. But why? Now, as they stood outside the diner, Serenity was trying to decide where she was going, trying not to admit to herself that she had enjoyed herself with Alex, despite the reason for their meeting.

"I guess I'll go help out at the nursery until later today when I can go back to my house. Unless you want me to go with you if you are interviewing anyone else today."

Alex was tempted to say yes, but he had no one else to talk to. It was time for him to just start praying that something would turn up that he hadn't known about yet. As she turned to go, Serenity looked back into the diner and saw Betty Jean and Joseph watching them. When she waved and smiled at the two of them, Joseph scowled and turned away as Betty Jean smiled and waved back.

Still smiling at Betty Jean, Serenity whispered to Alex, "Have you noticed how much the two of them have been watching us?"

Alex took her arm and turned his back to the diner to walk her to her car and said, "Yes. What do you think that's about?"

As she slid into her car, Alex leaning on the door frame, she said, "I think they know something and are afraid we'll figure it out."

Alex nodded as he closed her door. He agreed. But what did they know? Perhaps Betty Jean was only sharing his blush with Joseph, and the two of them were laughing at him because his crush on Serenity was so apparent. Or perhaps the two of them knew much more than they were saying about the missing boys. Something told him it was both things.

As Serenity drove away, Alex couldn't shake the feeling that they were on the cusp of uncovering something big. He watched her car disappear around the corner, then turned back to the diner. Through the window, he saw Betty Jean and Joseph in deep conversation, their faces serious. He made a mental note to keep a closer eye on those two. In a town like Lazy Rivers, everyone had secrets. But some secrets, he was beginning to realize, were far more dangerous than others.

With a heavy sigh, Alex headed to his patrol car. The case of the missing boys was far from over, and he had a feeling that before it was solved, many more secrets would come to light—some of which could change Lazy Rivers forever. And him. He didn't know if that was a good or bad thing. He had never wanted to care enough about someone to worry about them, and now he did.

What if after they solved the mystery of the missing boys—they had to there was no way around that—and Lizzy Rivers got better, would Serenity leave town? Or would he ask her to stay? It was the first time since his brother went missing that he felt afraid of losing someone. It wasn't a good feeling at all.

Forty

John had literally run away when Mama found him standing by the tree. The shock of seeing her momentarily overriding all rational thought. Of course he never called her Mama. She had earned that name over the years, caring for the nursery and anyone who came into her presence that needed help. Her name was Ruth, and that's what he said when he heard someone step into the clearing and had turned and saw her. "Ruth."

All of their history came flooding back, and he went into fight or flight mode. He chose flight. Leaving her standing in the clearing, waiting for him to say something else, he turned away and left, out through the edge of the nursery to his car parked along the side of the road.

He had come that way so he wouldn't see anyone. Especially Ruth. What he wanted to know was if the symbol was still on the tree. And of course it was.

He hoped that he would handle showing up at Elizabeth Rivers house better than what he had just done in the woods. *Running away. Good God, what was that about?* He prayed that Lizzy wasn't home. He couldn't handle seeing one more person from his past.

Going to the house was bad enough. As kids, they sometimes played there. Lizzy's mother, Mae, was always standing in the upstairs window watching them. Never smiling. It was a wonder that Lizzy actually learned to smile in that atmosphere.

Of course they all knew they were taking a chance playing near and with Rivers women. They could read your mind. That's what he had thought until ten-year-old Lizzy set him straight.

"I can't read your mind, dumb-dumb; I can only see stuff you remember. And I just saw a memory for the first time last week, so I haven't seen any of your stupid ones anyway."

"What memory can you see then?" he had asked, more curious than anything else. She had squinted up her face pretending to try to see something and then laughed.

"I can't just see something because I want to. It just happens."

Ruth had been with them that day, as she almost always was, and he remembered being glad that Lizzy couldn't see his memory of the first time he saw Ruth. It was stupid really, but he had thought she was the most amazing girl ever when he had seen her climb a tree faster than anyone else. Plus, she was smart. Smarter than him. And at least he was smart enough to know that was a good thing.

As he drove, John allowed himself to remember all the fun times they had spent together. If he was going to cry about it, he was going to do it in the car before he saw his son and had to pretend that everything was normal. As a kid, he had always thought that he and Ruth would end up together. They dated, if that's what it was called, starting in junior high. And in their senior year, they were planning what university they would go to so they could stay together.

And then Ruth got a part-time job at Tate's Nursery and met Ted Tate. He was ten years older. A grown man. Tall, blond, tan, and good-looking. Once Ruth met him, his dreams of their being together vanished almost over night.

She cried when she broke up with him. He got mad. But eventually he realized if he wanted to see her at all, he had to be okay with just being friends. He got good at pretending to be happy for her when she and Ted married—way too young, everyone said—but then Ruth reminded everyone that Ted wasn't too young, and that's what counted. Not long after that, Ruth got pregnant. And that was that.

Still, John had stayed close to Ruth and, of course, Lizzy, since they were a package. Sometimes he helped out the nursery. And that's how the three of them were together that day. He saw the man carve something in the tree trunk. And it was his curiosity that turned that sighting into something that changed his life. And after that, he couldn't stay in Lazy Rivers without thinking about what had happened, afraid he'd tell Ruth. Afraid that Lizzy would see the memory.

And he was still scared about that. Randy had told him that Lizzy had a daughter and a granddaughter. Three times the chance that one of them would see what actually happened the day Zach went missing. He had to ask himself why he had come back. Maybe he wanted to be caught. Even though he had a good life, meeting his beautiful, much younger wife many years after leaving Lazy Rivers and having a great son like Randy, what had happened haunted him.

Perhaps it was time to bring it out into the open. Especially since Randy had told him there was another missing boy. Although he couldn't see how that had anything to do with Zach. That was fifty years ago. How could it be happening now? John glanced at the scar on his left arm. The one he had made on purpose to cover what was there. He had tried to erase the past, but maybe he had learned too late that you can't.

"The past seeps into the present and colors the future." That's what his mother used to tell him. How right she was. She had always told him to learn from the past and then let it go. He had learned alright. He just hadn't let it go.

Driving up the rutted lane to the Rivers home, he shook his head. What a mess. *How could they have let their property and house get this way? The same way you ignored what needed to be fixed,* he said to himself. It seemed appropriate to him that the Rivers women were fixing up what they had, and he intended to fix what he had done. He just wasn't sure how to do that yet.

As he rounded the bend, he saw Randy walking around the side of the house. He waved, and John's heart grew lighter. He hadn't seen Randy for almost four years. He had wasted all these years feeling sorry for himself after his wife died. Randy had moved on and made a life for himself. And now he was inviting him to join him.

He was a lucky man. He still had a chance to make things right, with his son and with the town of Lazy Rivers. And Ruth. Ruth most of all. He had heard her husband died. Now they had that in common, too. Tomorrow he'd go see her, tell her what he knew, and ask her to help. For now, he'd enjoy the gift of working again with his son.

Yep, that's what I'll do, John said to himself as he stepped out of the truck and went to hug his son. Tomorrow would come soon enough.

Forty One

"Shall we go together?" Sam asked Matthew. "Or at least arrive together?"

The two of them had spent the last hour talking. Matthew had never stopped smiling. Samantha had alternated between smiling and crying. It was surreal. This was a man who knew her grandmother. Not just knew her, loved her. And if she had it right, since Rivers women mated until they got pregnant, he was her grandfather.

"How can that be?" she had asked. "How could you know my grandmother? How long did you know her?"

Matthew told her the story of arriving in town and falling head over heels in love with Elizabeth Rivers and thinking she loved him back. Then, six months later, she had forced him to leave. Made him promise to never come back. Lizzy told him she had seen a memory of him and his first love kissing, and she couldn't stay with him anymore. Arguing that it had been years earlier hadn't moved her at all. She remained resolute. She packed his bags and practically pushed him out the door.

Matthew hadn't known about the mating history of Rivers women. He hadn't known that she had used him to get pregnant and then made him leave. He didn't know he had a daughter named Serenity.

"Did she do the same thing?" Matthew had asked. Sam knew what he meant. Did Serenity get pregnant and push Sam's father out the door?

"Of course she did," Sam replied. "I don't know who my father is."

But then, seeing Matthew's kind face, she reached out and held his hands. "But I now know you are my grandfather. We can prove it. We can ask Lizzy."

"I can't," Matthew had said.

"You're angry, and you have a right to be. But she was only doing what she was told to do. I will not do that, by the way. I will not get married. I'm never having a child. I'm going to stop this gift right now."

Matthew's face had softened at her words. "Why Sam? We all have gifts that sometimes get in the way. You have learned to live with it. Pick a man who could live with it too. I would have stayed with Lizzy. Lived with that gift, put up with her seeing memories, good or bad. Just to be with her. Find a man like that and have a life."

Sam had broken down then, and he had held her hand until the tears stopped, thinking that the universe had given him the greatest gift of all. One he had never even dreamed of having. Someone like Sam to love. And he had a daughter. And Lizzy was still alive. Just. That's why Samantha was in town—to see her ill grandmother. She had stalled out in Spring Falls but was heading to Lazy Rivers now. And he had to go, too. No matter what Lizzy had wanted in the past, he had to see her before she died.

"We both have a car, so we'll have to arrive together," had been his answer.

"Lunch first?" Sam said, "I'm so hungry. Not a good idea to see mom when I'm hungry."

As they walked to ParaTi's, Sam pointed out the gallery where she thought her mom could display some of her paintings.

"Your mother's an artist?" Matthew asked, thinking that it was magical that he would have an artist for a daughter.

"A famous one," Samantha replied. "But as you can imagine, she is a recluse, so only a few people know who she is. She doesn't sign the paintings with her last name."

Matthew stopped in the middle of the sidewalk, thinking of a painting he had seen in a New York gallery. It took up almost half the wall. Filled with trees, mist, and colors that looked as if the flowers had come alive and filled all the empty spaces. Barely there, like a sighing breeze.

He had stood in front of that painting, thinking that if he ever stayed in one place, he would like to own it. Every day, he could disappear into that beauty. Now he remembered looking at the name of the artist and thinking that whoever had painted it had painted a picture of her name—Serenity.

Watching Matthew's face, Sam laughed. "You've seen one of her paintings."

"I have. In New York. It was magnificent. My daughter?"

"Looks that way."

Seeing Matthew's face and his joy at learning he had a daughter made Sam think about her mother differently. What would it be like to meet her without the history of growing up with her? That's when she fully understood that she didn't really know her mother. She wondered if anyone did know their parents. Did anyone take the time to re-meet the people that raised them without the history of the past in the way?

One reason she didn't want children was that she knew she'd be a terrible mother. She liked things her way. She didn't like being told what to do or how to do it. Freedom could be her middle name.

Which meant, in reverse, she must have been a difficult child to raise. And yet she was healthy and successful. Some of that must have been because Serenity had done everything she knew how to make sure that Sam could be successful in the world.

I've misjudged her, Samantha thought. Perhaps it had been a mistake to stay away. But it was the same mistake her mother made with her mother, and who knows how many before them? *Matthew is right. It's time to break this cycle.*

"Are you okay?" Matthew asked. They were still standing on the sidewalk as people walked around them. Sam having stopped to think about her mother as Matthew took in the fact he had an artist for a daughter.

Overhead, the sun peaked out from the clouds drifting across the sky, the light filtering through the poplar tree, making a moving pattern on the sidewalk. It reminded her of Lazy Rivers and the trees that graced their streets. Two pretty towns so close to each other. How did that happen?

"Yes," Samantha said, hooking her arm into her grandfather's. "Let's get something to eat and then go freak out a few Rivers women."

"Sounds like a plan," Matthew answered. "And we best plan how we are going to do that freaking out. I'd like to be invited to stay after that."

"Good point," Sam answered, thinking how their showing up together could all go wrong. And for the first time, she wanted it to all go right. She was tired of running away. She was ready to go home.

<h1 style="text-align:center">Forty Two</h1>

After watching Serenity and Alex drive away, Betty Jean turned from the window and looked up at Joseph. All these years later, she still had that moment of joy that he was there. And even now, knowing that they were in trouble, that joy sparked for a moment.

Joseph didn't say anything. She didn't expect him to. He wasn't a talkative man. He wasn't all that nice of a man to other people either. At least that's what he wanted people to believe. And to do that, he acted in ways that scared people. Just a little.

Well, sometimes a lot, she admitted to herself. She remembered the first time she saw him when she came to the diner looking for a job. One she had to have or she'd be eating out of garbage cans. She figured at least she'd have food, and she could sleep in the car if necessary. It was an old beater. One that had sat in the yard of their house for years, only because her dad was too lazy to get rid of it. Or too drunk. She didn't know which came first.

Then he died. She found him behind the house. At first Betty Jean thought he had passed out, as he often did. And then she was relieved. It wasn't as if he had been there for her. She never knew her mother. She had been told she died when she was born. Because she had no choice, she had to believe that. Otherwise she'd have to be mad at her for leaving her with such a cruel man.

But a few days later, the owner of the house had arrived and kicked her out. She was eighteen, on her own, and homeless. Which is how she found herself at the diner looking for work. And it was why, even with Joseph towering over her, he didn't scare her. She knew what scary men felt like, and for some reason he hadn't felt the same.

He said he didn't need help. She looked around the diner at people waiting for their order to be taken and said, "Yes, you do."

The plan was to stay for a little while, earn enough money to get out of town, and never look back. But here she was, all these years later, and she had never left. She had earned enough money to buy herself a small house in town. And she no longer drove a beater. It was used, but it ran well, and it was hers.

Truthfully, she had stayed for Joseph. A big hulk of a man running a business that he was expected to run and scaring everyone away on purpose. Everyone but her. She understood what he was capable of, and yet she stayed. She knew people thought the two of them were together but couldn't prove it, and they both liked it that way. Sometimes when he was out of town on business, he was out of town in her home, where he was a different man.

Now, though, looking up at him, Betty Jean wondered if what they had done was the right thing. Both of them looked down at his left arm and thought about what was underneath his shirt. Of course she recognized the symbol when Alex had shown it to her. She had almost dropped the coffee pot, but years of practice kept her standing there, smiling, pretending that she didn't know. Acting innocent.

"I hear you are going out of town," Betty Jean said to Joseph. Just loud enough to be heard.

No one needed to hear Joseph's answer. They wouldn't have anyway, because all he did was nod at her. But she knew he understood. They needed to talk. He'd be at her house when her shift ended. Despite her years of handling everything that came her way, Betty Jean was afraid. Alex and Serenity were going to figure it out. And then what were they going to do?

The rest of the afternoon dragged on. Joseph had left. Simply turned away from the front door and gone out the back, saying nothing to anyone. Now it was up to Betty Jean to run the restaurant, something she had been doing for years. When it was time for her to go home, the night manager would come on. Since Joseph didn't have a son to leave the diner to or to train to run the restaurant, he had been searching for a long time for someone to replace him.

So far, the new kid was doing well. He only worked for a few hours. The diner closed at nine, but it was enough to see that he might work out. Which relieved Betty Jean. She was reaching the time of her life when working a ten-hour shift six days a week was getting to be too much. She was looking forward to turning the diner over to someone else.

"Why don't you want kids?" she had asked Joseph at one time, knowing it would be her to have them and not sure she wanted any either. "They'd be trapped in the diner, just like I am," he had answered.

She knew that was ridiculous. Or she felt it was. He could have sold the diner. The outside business of selling sauces did well enough to support him. But he had told his father he would, and there was no way he wouldn't keep his promise to his dad. That was Joseph. A man who kept his feelings to himself, who was more private than anyone she had ever met, who was loyal to a fault even when he was wrong, and who knew how to run a business.

And she loved him. That made all of what they had done together both easier and harder. Because she just couldn't lose him now, and when Alex figured it out, that was a possibility. She couldn't let that happen. Finally, the clock said she could go home. After making sure all was taken care of with the night manager and waitress, she walked out the back door to her car.

Turning right and right again heading home, she passed the diner just in time to see two cars pull up, and the drivers get out. She thought she recognized the man and the woman who stepped out, but then thought that couldn't be. That couldn't be Lizzy's granddaughter, and for sure that couldn't be Lizzy's Matthew. Men were so hard to tell apart as they got older, but he sure walked like him.

Impossible. How could they be together? Besides, she had bigger problems than trying to figure out who those two people could be. She'd find out tomorrow. In the meantime, she and Joseph needed to figure out what to do next. No decision was going to feel good. But one needed to be made.

Forty Three

After her meeting with Alex, Serenity went to the nursery to see her mom and to help, thinking working outside might help clear her thinking. She found Lizzy in the office sorting through old files, scanning them, and putting them into the computer. After they broke the task up into one of them scanning and the other making sure they went into the right folder in the computer, it moved much faster.

After an hour of working together, Lizzy said she was tired and done for the day and asked Serenity to take her to Mama's house. They looked for Mama but didn't see her, so they told Tom where they were going. He hadn't seen his mother either, but said when she turned up he'd let her know that Lizzy had gone to the house.

After dropping Lizzy off at Mama's house and making sure she had everything she needed, Serenity headed for home. Yes, it would be a mess, but she wanted to make sure everything was going to plan. She also wanted a chance to go over details with either Randy or Brad. Or both. Maybe her studio would be done enough that she could start painting again.

As she drove, she wondered where Mama had gone off to. It wasn't like her to not be around checking on everyone. Maybe she was working somewhere in the back of the nursery. Serenity had linked her phone to the car, and Willie Nelson was playing softly in the background as her thoughts drifted towards the man Mama had seen at the nursery so many years before. The one she said the plants had moved away from. Who had that been? And did it have anything to do with the missing boys?

As Willie sang, "Always On My Mind," she reviewed what had happened since she had come home. Life in Lazy Rivers was entirely different from the one she had been living, alone with her painting. Different and surprisingly good, and she found it disturbing that a missing boy was making things better for her.

She had enjoyed herself with Alex, and the memories she had seen of the people around her had been easier to handle. Mostly because they were either something simple, like washing dishes, or they felt unreal, like a dream. She hoped that the trend would continue.

Do you want both trends to continue? She asked herself. *Alex and softening memories?* She didn't answer herself. It was too complicated. A few minutes later she was bouncing through ruts and potholes on the drive up to the house.

She needed to have Randy level it out. She was sure the drive would get worse over the winter if it wasn't fixed. As she rounded the curve and could see the house, she saw all the trucks parked out front, and she could see workers everywhere. But there was one she didn't recognize at all. It occurred to her it might be Randy's dad.

She parked her car far enough away to not get in the way of the workers, or anyone leaving, and went looking for Randy, or Brad. Either would do. It was Brad who found her standing in the middle of the living room with her hands over her ears coughing at the dust, ready to cry at the mess.

"Here," he said, handing her a hard hat and goggles, and leading her back outside. "You don't want to be walking through construction sites without these."

She put them on and coughed. "And you might want to wear a mask too," he added.

Then, noticing her tears he led her further away from the noise and confusion.

"It won't look like this in a few days," he said.

"It just took me by surprise," Serenity said, pulling a tissue out of her pocket and dabbing at her eyes, glad she wasn't wearing makeup or it would be running down her face. "I know you need to make a mess to clean something up, or make it better, but this was a bigger mess than I expected."

Brad nodded. "And louder, I expect. But Randy is doing a great job keeping it together. I just stopped by to make sure everything was going well, and it is. So far no surprises. We'll be done for the day in an hour, and most of the dust will be gone with us. Randy has people cleaning up as they go, knowing that you are living here. He's a good kid. Speaking of Randy, that's his dad."

Serenity looked up to see a tall thin man, wearing a well used tool belt, heading to the truck she had thought might be his. It was strange to think that he had been friends with her mom and Mama, and then left and never come back. Now he had returned, because his son was here, and he was working on her mother's house. Why had all these things lined up like that? Was it all because of the missing boy? Did John Carver returning home have something to do with that?

Randy came up behind his dad, put his arm around him and the two of them stood by the truck, talking. Watching them, Serenity thought that they probably had a lot to catch up on, like her and her mother. She hadn't been gone from Lazy Rivers as long as Randy's dad, but still she hadn't been here. Now they were all returning home. Including Sam. She hadn't heard from her, but she knew somehow that she was on her way.

Perhaps then three of them could work together to discover where Jimmy Hunter had gone and maybe solve the mystery of the other three boys. If they were alive, they would be men by now of course, but still. She had just read a story about a man who was found sixty-one years after being kidnapped from his home. Anything was possible.

She was smiling at the thought when she saw a memory. *Whose memory is this?* she asked herself. There were so many people around it could be anyone's. But then she saw the oak tree and a man carving the symbol on it. She let the memory play, looking for clues both for who the man at the tree was and whose memory it was; it had to be someone old enough to be there. And that's when she realized it was John Carver's memory.

He had been there with Mama and Lizzy. Why hadn't they said so the first time they talked about it? Is that why he left town? If only the man would turn around, she could sketch a picture of his face and show it to people. She was sure all of this went together, all she had to do was put the pieces in place.

John Carver, feeling as if someone had just looked inside of him, turned to see a woman standing with Brad. He had never met her, but he knew who she had to be. It was the same feeling he had when Lizzy saw his memories. This had to be Lizzy's daughter. But what did she see? Had she figured out what he knew?

Once again, he wanted to run, just as he had done fifty years before, and again today running from Ruth. But this time, he knew he couldn't. And despite what that could mean, he felt relief. It would soon be over.

Forty Four

Mama Tate had been on her way back from the oak tree when she saw Serenity arrive. Instead of doing the normal thing—going to meet with her, maybe spending some time talking—she had done the exact opposite. She had turned away and headed back to the tree, and then followed the path that John Carver had taken to the back road. Not thinking. Just moving. Once she reached the gravel road, she stopped and looked for his truck.

She knew he'd be driving a truck. At sixteen, he had gotten his first one; it was old and battered, but it was his. Even then, he had tools in the back, ready to work. She supposed he got into the habit from his dad. And now Randy had followed in their footsteps. The Carver men, always working some kind of construction. Always fixing things to make them better. And then, of course, there were the Rivers women. What did they do? Fix things? No, they had not, given the way they had behaved in the generations that she knew of.

But Mama knew that was changing. They were willing to see memories now and use their gift rather than running from it. Mama wondered if it was ever possible to run from the gifts you have been given. One way or another, gifts make themselves known, and everyone has to learn to live with them. When she was in high school, there was a beautiful girl that all the boys practically panted over when she was around. Mama remembered standing in the hallway watching them flock around the girl, feeling jealous, when one of her favorite teachers came up and stood beside her.

"Being beautiful is a gift," she had said, "but it is also a burden. And with it comes a choice of using it for good or evil."

Mama had never been jealous of that girl again. And because of what her teacher said, she saw what that girl had to put up with, whether or not she liked it. Later, she remembered what her teacher had said, realizing that it applied to all gifts. Now, older than her teacher had been, she was even more aware of the potential of all gifts being a burden, depending on how they were used. If you didn't use gifts correctly, they haunted you.

But what is my gift? It was the question she had asked herself that day and was still asking. She wasn't beautiful. She couldn't see memories like Lizzy or fix things like John. The thought occurred to her she didn't have a gift. But she knew that wasn't possible. At least in her version of the world it wasn't. She wasn't religious, but she believed in an existing goodness. Some kind of intelligence had put the universe together, and that intelligence had to be love and goodness. Because the world was beautiful.

Maybe not what humans did to it, but beauty and kindness were its essence, even though it was often buried under garbage. She hadn't run a nursery all these years without seeing the beauty and order that underlay everything. That was what she believed and counted on, because despite all the greed and power struggles that existed, her world view, the only one that made sense, was that good always prevailed. Believing that, she knew that the divine good intelligence that was love wouldn't have designed anything without giving it a gift.

Which meant her too. So what was her gift? Being a motherhen? Maybe. If so, she wasn't doing such a good job of it, hiding out here in the back of their property, looking for a truck she knew wouldn't be there.

Although she had broken up with John Carver soon after she met Ted Tate—no one else stood a chance—she and John had stayed friends. Until that day at the tree. The three of them together, both her and Lizzy barely pregnant.

They had told John that secret as they walked. She had waited to tell him until she had Lizzy with her. She knew, although he had told her he was fine with her marrying Ted, that the pregnancy would hurt him. So she softened it, she hoped, by them both telling him about how wonderful it felt to be pregnant at the same time as her best friend.

John hadn't said anything. He had stopped for a moment. Looked down. And then started walking again. He walked a little faster than them, so eventually he was so far ahead they could barely see his plaid jacket and the old hat he wore which she knew had the logo of the chainsaw he used on it.

"I guess he didn't take it well," Lizzy had said. Surprising herself, Mama had cried, and they stopped for a minute while she pulled herself together.

"I want him to be happy for me, but is that fair?" she had asked.

Lizzy hadn't answered because they both knew there wasn't an answer that would make it any easier. As they started walking again, they saw John walking toward them. At first, Mama thought he was coming to say something to her about the baby, but instead he put his finger on his lips and said, "Shh... There is someone at the oak tree."

The three of them made their way silently to the edge of the clearing and watched as the man stood at the tree, carving something on it.

Now, standing on the gravel road, Mama thought back to that day. Maybe her gift, or the gift all of them had, was the gift of keeping a secret. But if it was a gift, they had used it the wrong way that day. All three of them had watched, not saying anything. Then, as the man walked to the back of the property towards the same gravel road that she was standing on now, Lizzy said, "Isn't that the guy who owns the diner?"

It was then that Mama realized that was the same man that the plants had reacted to. He was big and scary, so they kept that secret of what they had seen. *What good would it do to ruin his life?* they had thought. Just because the plants moved away from him and he carved something on a tree. So what? It hadn't seemed all that important that day. And besides, he had frightened them, and they had to live in the same town as he did. He knew who they were.

How were they to know then that the symbol had something to do with Zach going missing? What worried her though, was why John Carver left not long after that. Zach went missing, and John moved away, never even coming by the nursery to say goodbye. She had always thought it was because he couldn't stay in town anymore because of her. But maybe it was more than that.

And that's why she was afraid now. John had run from her. What secret was he keeping? And what if Joseph Tate knew why his father carved a symbol on an oak tree and never said anything? And, what did it mean? His father couldn't be responsible for the boys that were missing. He had died years before, so it couldn't have been him who put that same symbol out at the old house. Who had done that?

Was it Joseph? And then what did that mean? The only thing Ruth knew for sure was that it was time to figure it all out. Now that John was in town, it was time for all three of them to tell someone what they knew. But first she'd talk to Lizzy, and they'd decide together.

Forty Five

A young man greeted Sam and Matthew as they came in the diner's door, both of them looking around for anyone they might know.

"Sit wherever you like," he said.

Matthew smiled and asked if Betty Jean or Joseph were there.

"Nope, they both just left. How do you know them?"

"I used to live here, long before you were born," Matthew said, laughing and enjoying the way the young man looked at Sam. Yes, his granddaughter was quite beautiful. Just then, Betty Jean walked in through the kitchen.

"Forgot something," she said, reaching under the counter to get the dinners she had put there for herself and Joseph.

Then she looked up at the two people standing there, put the dinners down, and ran out from behind the counter to greet Matthew.

"Matthew Nelson, as I live and breathe. I never thought I would see you again!"

Turning to the woman standing beside him, she asked, "And you're Samantha Rivers, aren't you? All grown up and so beautiful."

And then her hands flew to her mouth as she said, "Oh," realizing what that meant.

"Yes, oh," Matthew laughed. "We just met, actually. And we're hungry."

By then, the few people in the diner were actively watching and listening, so Betty Jean turned and looked at everyone in the room. With her hands on her hips, she said, "If any of you breathe a word to anyone else about this until these two see Lizzy Rivers you won't be allowed in the diner for a year. You understand?"

Everyone nodded and laughed a little, knowing that Betty Jean wasn't kidding.

A man at the counter yelled out, "Well, tell her soon then!"

Matthew turned to him, recognized Pete, and answered with a smile, "Right after we eat!"

After Betty Jean seated the two of them, Sam leaned forward and whispered to Matthew, "Really? Right after we eat?"

Matthew gestured to the people in the diner. "How long do you think it would take for this news to spread?"

Which is why forty minutes later, they were on the way to Lizzy's house. Although they were both hungry, they hadn't eaten much, both of them too nervous about what would happen when they saw Lizzy.

At first, they couldn't even decide how to do it. Should they go together? Should Sam go first and prepare the way? All they knew for sure was that it had to be done. The question was how.

Betty Jean had hugged them both before she left with her dinners, and told them not to worry, they would be welcome. Despite that, they weren't sure. Of course, Sam would be welcome, but what about Matthew? And how would everyone feel about the fact that they had met? It was a secret before, and now it wasn't.

In the end, they went in separate cars. Matthew knew no matter what, he couldn't stay at the house and would have to find a place in town. As they drove down the rutted road to her family's home, Sam leading the way, they passed a line of trucks leading away from the house. *What's going on?* Sam asked herself. As they passed she looked at the drivers but didn't know anyone.

There were still two trucks left at the house and two men talking at the door of one. Who were these people and why were they there? And why was there a dumpster in the yard? Was her grandmother selling the house? Had they already moved? Surely they would have told her.

She didn't remember the house being so old. Is that why the trucks were there? Were they fixing it or tearing it down? At the moment, it wasn't clear. Both she and Matthew just stood there not knowing what to do next.

Then her mother was running out of the house, and at that moment Samantha realized how much she had missed her and started running too. The two of them met in the yard, hugging and laughing.

"Oh my gosh, Sam, you look so beautiful," Serenity said, holding her at arms length to take her all in.

Sam looked back at her mother with tears in her eyes, and when she saw tears in her mother's eyes, the woman who tried to never cry in front of everyone, she realized how stupid it had been for her to stay away.

"You look beautiful too, mom!" Another brief hug and then Serenity asked, "Did that man come with you? Who is he?"

"Oh," Sam said. For a moment she had forgotten who was with her.

Matthew had watched his daughter and granddaughter hug, and tried not to cry himself. To distract himself and to give them time together, he turned to the men at the truck who were watching. As he walked toward them he realized he knew one of them. Extending his hand he said, "John Carver!'

"Matthew, is that you? I thought it might be, but what are you doing here?"

"I could ask you the same thing. Do you still live in Lazy Rivers?"

"No, but my son moved here and I'm visiting."

That was when the two of them turned to Randy, who had not paid any attention to his father or the stranger. Instead, he was staring at Sam as if he had been struck by lighting. The two men looked at each other and laughed. They recognized that look. Both of them had it at one time in their life.

By then, Serenity and Sam had reached the two men, and John introduced his son to Matthew and Sam.

"Hi," Sam said, trying to stop herself from staring at Randy. She recognized him from somewhere. Besides, he hadn't stopped staring at her either. It was weird. But she was more worried about what to do next. She had a bigger problem than a strange man who looked familiar. She had to introduce her mother to her father.

But Serenity had already figured it out. She saw Matthew's memory of meeting her mother, and them laughing together in the house. Besides, she recognized the eyes looking at her with love in them. They were the same eyes that she saw every time she looked in a mirror.

Frozen in time, she waited. How did she feel about meeting her father? She could tell how he felt. It was radiating from him in waves of love and joy. How could she resist that? She couldn't, really.

Matthew must have known she had seen who he was because he simply stood and waited for her to say something. It was her choice about what to do next.

After what seemed hours but was really only a few seconds, Serenity took a deep breath and said, "I'm not sure what to say about meeting the man who is my father, but here you are, and obviously you two have a story to share, and I want to hear it. Randy and John, would you join us?"

Randy didn't have to be asked twice. He had stood watching everything, barely able to speak. Now he'd have a chance to redeem himself. Or try to anyway.

John hesitated. He knew what was happening. This was the beginning of the unraveling, but that was what he had come to Lazy Rivers to do. Put things right, maybe help find the missing boy. He had wanted to tell the secret, and it looked as if this was where he would begin.

As they walked to the house, Sam glanced back at Randy, and then remembered where she had seen those eyes. It was one of the reasons she had not stopped in Lazy Rivers and went to Spring Falls instead.

How weird was it that he'd be here at her mother's house?

Well, considering that I ended up staying at the same motel as my grandfather, I guess it's not so weird at that, she thought.

Serenity was having the same kind of thoughts. *How did her father end up with her daughter? And what in God's name would her mother think?* And what really worried her was the other memory she had just seen of John Carver watching the man at the tree. Did her father know about it too? Her head hurt just thinking about it, and the desire to run was strong.

But her daughter had come home. Her father had returned, and although she wasn't sure how she felt about having a father after all these years, he was here now. And there was still a missing boy. How did they all fit together? She couldn't run away this time. Instead, she'd have to figure it out.

Forty Six

Joseph was at her house when Betty Jean got home. She expected him to be. It was why she had prepared two dinners. And then forgotten them at the diner. But she supposed that was what was meant to be.

Otherwise, she wouldn't have discovered that Sam and Matthew had come to town. Like thunderclouds before a rain, there was a gathering of people. Samantha, Matthew, John, and Serenity had all come home. They probably didn't realize what that meant—a storm was brewing. But Betty Jean could see it coming.

As each person returned home, it felt like a lightning strike, and you could gauge how close the storm was by counting the seconds until thunder was heard. And it all centered around what had happened fifty years before.

Well, before that. But she and Joseph hadn't been part of that then. For them, it all began fifty years ago when Zach went missing.

It was a long-held secret, one they had kept, but now it was time to tell it. But how? And to whom?

She and Joseph would have to decide together, and when they did, nothing would be the same. The question was, would the storm bring a gentle cleansing rain or a flood washing away everything?

Joseph was waiting for her in her tiny living room. She loved her house, tucked away behind a stand of thuja and white pine trees. In the yard, a redbud tree bloomed every spring, and seeing it always made her heart sing.

When she wasn't working at the diner, she gardened. Every year she tried to make the house and the garden prettier. Now the daffodils were gone, and summer flowers were starting to bloom. Although sometimes she brought flowers into the house, she mostly left them alone. During summer evenings, she and Joseph would sit outside and enjoy the garden and the privacy the trees brought them.

Inside, her house smelled like whatever wax she had melting in the wax warmer. Today the scent was vanilla caramel spice. She could smell it even in the garage as she stepped out of her car. It always made them both smile to come home to a lovely aroma. Today, it didn't seem to have done much for Joseph. He was not smiling.

Years before, to make him comfortable in her house, she had bought oversized chairs and a large couch. And then she added an enormous bed that took up most of her bedroom. But she had never cared. She would trade everything for time with him, which was pretty much what she had done. No children and a secret life. All for Joseph.

But coming home and finding him in her house was something she loved. He'd be sitting in the big comfy chair waiting for her, maybe with a cup of coffee beside him and almost always with a book in his hands. Well, not an actual book anymore. These days he read on his iPad.

"There's no need to have stuff around, and besides, this way I always have a book with me," he had said when she had asked him about changing to digital books. "Besides, it gives me lots of books to read all in one place."

He had started out with an eReader, but it was so small in his big hands that he gave it up and switched to the bigger pad. She wasn't much of a reader herself, but she loved having Joseph tell her about the stories he had read. He wasn't reading today, though. He was brooding, his tall frame slumped in the chair. That was the best word for it, she thought. Angry? Sad? No. Brooding. And instead of a welcoming smile, she saw sadness in his eyes.

Sitting down in the other chair that looked like his but was smaller so she wouldn't be swallowed up in it, she spun the chair so she was looking at him.

"You'll never guess who was in the diner." She didn't really expect him to answer; she knew they would have to address the thing that was bothering him, but for now this was the news. "Samantha Rivers and Matthew Nelson."

Betty Jean didn't know what she expected from Joseph, but it wasn't what she got. Nothing. He didn't move. She wasn't sure he even blinked. Instead, he just sat there, not looking at her. Following what he was staring at, she saw the picture of the three of them sitting on the table beside the fireplace.

She loved that fireplace. Joseph had fitted it with a woodstove so that when they built a fire, it warmed the entire house instead of all the heat going up the chimney. He kept them well stocked in firewood, and she loved their nights by the fire, him reading and her knitting, always keeping him at the corner of her vision, just in case he needed something.

They sometimes talked together, but they didn't need to. They had years of conversations and quiet times between them. Thousands of hours of treasured minutes. In all her daydreams as a young girl, she had never imagined this future. But the minute she had walked into the diner to look for a job, she had fallen for him. Standing beside his father. Handsome. Silent.

At the time, she had known it was impossible. He would never notice her. He was ten years older. And so much bigger than her. He was quiet. And a little scary. She didn't know then that he liked being perceived as scary. It kept people away. He had always kept people away. Later, he said that she had scared him when she walked in the door.

"You? Scared? Of me?" She had laughed, thinking he was kidding.

"Yes. I felt something. And that meant things would change. I don't like change. Besides, I had a secret, and you might not want to be part of it. So I almost didn't hire you."

"But you did," she had smiled, hugging him as she sat on his lap. To her, he was a gentle giant.

"How could I not?" he answered. "You needed a job. I needed a waitress. And I needed to watch over you."

"Even if I hadn't loved you back?" She had said, holding his face in her hands and staring into his hazel eyes.

"Even then," he had said. But she had, and that was the end of that. They had been together for all these years. Secretly and happily. And now it might come to an end. It depended on how they handled what needed to be done.

The picture Joseph was staring at had been taken a few years after she had come to work. They were standing with Joseph's father, who had an arm around them both, although he couldn't really put an arm around her. She was too small, and he was too tall. Instead, his hand rested on her shoulder. She could still feel the weight of his hand. That was the day Joseph's father had told them his secret. The one he had asked them to keep, and they agreed. Until now.

Michael Trapp was not someone you didn't want to agree with. Big Mike was his nickname, and he lived up to it. He was larger than life, and everything went his way. It was why Joseph had taken over the diner. It was why they both had said yes to his plan.

Big Mike was not someone you crossed. And yet, under that outward scary appearance, beat a kind, if ruthless, heart. And when he believed in something, he made sure it happened. And what he had believed in had ruled their lives.

"Samantha Rivers and Matthew Nelson have come to town," Betty Jean repeated. "And I brought dinner."

Joseph turned to her and nodded. He knew what she was saying. They'd eat and talk and figure out what to do next. *What would Big Mike do?* he asked himself. Maybe he should do the exact opposite this time. This time, they'd tell.

Forty Seven

The decision to not let Matthew go see her mother was hers to make. She wasn't sorry about it. Matthew had been disappointed, and so was Sam. But Serenity thought that it would be too much. She'd tell Lizzy first. And she'd bring Sam. They'd see how Lizzy was doing and decide then. The story of how Sam and Matthew met in the hotel was so weird, it was hard to believe. All she could think was that something was directing what was happening.

She knew Mama believed in the hand of the Infinite guiding events, but she wasn't sure that she did. If that was so, then why all the bad things? Like boys going missing. What she couldn't decide was if Matthew coming home was a good or bad thing. That was her head talking. She knew that was why she was keeping him away from her mother for now.

But then her heart was talking too, but it kept going from happiness to sorrow. She had missed out on so many years with this man. Was that fair? Where was the Infinite, then? Because she thought they might have been good years. He was interesting, kind, or at least appeared that way. And obviously he loved her mother.

She should be mad at her mother, she thought. Sending him away. But then, hadn't she done the exact same thing? That was the Rivers Rule. Get pregnant; send the man away without him knowing a thing. *My decision was different,* she tried to reason with herself. She hadn't loved him. Nor did she think he loved her. It was a union only for the purpose of making a beautiful daughter. Of course, like Matthew, he had never known about it, and if she could help it, he never would.

Like Matthew, he was a nice man, but unlike Matthew, she knew that Lucas would never have wanted children. He had told her so. Which meant she had deceived him. *Who was the person who did wrong in this situation?* she asked herself. *What kind of person did that?* Plus, she reminded herself, Samantha had a right to know, too. Just like she did. And now that she knew who her father was, she understood what the not knowing had done. Could that ever be repaired? Maybe not.

She sighed, trying to not fall into the trap of shame, guilt, and self-pity. That would never help now. There were too many other things to worry about. She had no time to think of Sam's father, the father who had given Sam her long, dark hair and green eyes. But for the first time in her life, she considered trying to find Lucas. Not for her, or even for him. She'd do it for Sam.

Later, she said to herself. *One problem at a time.* And she had more than one. There was Matthew. The missing boy. The return of John Carver, which she was sure had something to do with the missing boy. But what? And her relationship with Sam. And then there was Alex. There was something between them. Maybe it had always been there. But that too needed to be addressed at another time and place.

The missing boy was the most important problem to solve. How did John Carver, Matthew, Sam, Alex, her mother, and Mama Tate figure into all of this, because she was sure they did.

And then, there was definitely something happening between Joseph and Betty Jean. Not just their relationship, which was obvious to anyone with half a mind to look, but something else. Oh, and then there were the looks passing between her daughter and Randy. What was that about?

And what about the house? Another immediate problem. The mess was everywhere, except her studio and the tiny room she had been sleeping in.

Before she sent Randy, John, and Matthew away, she had them help move her supplies into her studio and clean up the small room for Sam. They put a cot into the studio for her. She had used it when she was a girl, when she slept in the backyard, pretending to camp out.

As they moved things here and there, she felt like a mother hen clucking after the three of them. Or four of them. Samantha was as distracted as the men. But they finally got their rooms ready, and then the men were gone. And now there were two places in the house that weren't a mess.

One step at a time, and soon the house would be a wonderful place to live in, Serenity thought. Just like solving the problem of the missing boys one step at a time. They would do it, even though she knew at first it would be messy. She just wasn't sure how bad it would be.

She heard Randy invite Matthew to stay at his house with him and his dad, solving the problem of where Matthew would go. There was a motel just outside of town, but it wasn't very nice. They had a few BnBs, but it was too late to get into one now. So his offer was the perfect solution.

She agreed to meet Matthew again in the morning, back at the diner, and she'd let him know what happened with Lizzy and if it was okay to see her. "Besides," she had added, "You can tell me about yourself."

Matthew had smiled at her, and she saw why her daughter accepted him so readily. She had to. She just didn't want to admit it yet.

She and Sam had decided not to call ahead, although she had texted Tom and asked him where Mama and Lizzy were.

"What's up?" he had texted back.

"More than I can tell you now. Later though?"

"I'm all ears," he had replied, and he told them that both Mama and Lizzy were at Mama's house.

"Give us an hour or so and meet us there?"

After getting his thumbs up emoji, she and Sam changed out of their now dusty clothes and were on the road to Mama's. Serenity drove. Sam leaned out the window, swishing her hands in the air like she used to do as a child. Back then, it had scared Serenity and she had tried to get her to stop. But that had only made Sam more determined to do it. They'd argue. Sam would pout and not talk to her or give her the evil eye.

Now Serenity simply smiled. Keeping her mouth shut was something she had learned over the years. Sometimes she was successful at it. After a few minutes, Sam pulled her arms in and turned to her mother.

"Not going to stop me this time?"

"I'm just too happy to have you home. Besides, you're too big to fall out the window now, and I'm a little smarter than I used to be."

Sam's eyes teared, but she didn't want her mother to see. She had missed her so much. And now she was determined to get to know her mother as a person, not just as the woman who she knew had done her best to raise her. She reached across the seat to hold her mother's hand, and they both rode the rest of the way to Mama's house with tears in their eyes. Both of them refrained from asking each other the question, "How do you feel about Matthew?"

They might be in the middle of a gathering storm, but for now, they were content. *In the eye of the hurricane,* Serenity thought, determined to make the most of it. But when they pulled up in front of Mama's house, she could feel her heart beating so hard she put her hand up to her chest to try to calm down.

"It will be okay, mom," Sam said. "I'm scared about it too, but in the end, this is the best thing."

Serenity nodded and said, "I hope so."

And then Mama was there with a worried look on her face, and Serenity's heart beat even faster.

Forty Eight

"Is there something wrong with mom?" Serenity almost yelled. Not this. It would be too much.

"Oh no, honey," Mama said. "I just need to tell you something."

And then, seeing Sam, she squealed a little and ran to hug her. "Oh my gosh, you are a sight for sore eyes. Your grandmother is going to be so happy to see you."

And then, seeing both their faces, she stepped back. "What's happening?"

"We have something to tell you, too," Sam answered.

Mama ran her hand through her short gray hair, looked around her at the trees swaying with the breeze, her poppies and day lilies blooming beside the driveway, and took one deep breath of the sweet air before turning to lead them into the house. She knew by the time she walked Serenity and Sam back to their car, all of her world would have tilted a little. She wanted to remember how it used to be.

But then maybe it will be better, she thought to herself and then added, *Maybe in the long run, but it's going to be messy at first. Might as well get started.*

Just then, in the distance, she saw a lightning flash. Another storm was coming. In just a few seconds, the air had changed from sweet to the smell that proceeds a storm. *That's funny, God*, she whispered to herself. *Quite symbolic.* The three of them looked at each other and then laughed. The message was quite clear.

"The good thing about storms," Mama said, as they walked to the house, "is that they clear the air."

There was no time to say more because Lizzy had opened the front door and stood there beaming. Sam rushed into her arms, and as they hugged, she whispered she was sorry she hadn't come sooner.

"Everything in the right timing," Lizzy whispered back and hugged her granddaughter again, thinking how lucky she was to have her.

Sam hadn't seen Mama's house since she was a little girl and had forgotten how much her house and garden reflected Mama's love of plants. There were prayer plants and green vines hanging down from bookshelves that looked as if they were designed so that there could be pots of plants on them.

A huge rubber tree stood in the corner of the living room, and a massive coffee table sat in the middle of two dark gray couches with green throw pillows with a curvy leaf design on them tucked into the corners. A fluffy pink blanket lay over the arm of one of the two big chairs on the other side of the coffee table, and that's where Lizzy went to sit.

Serenity smiled. This was the perfect spot for her mother. There were books and drinks on a side table, and a bowl of almonds. No wonder her mother looked so much better.

Reading her mind, Lizzy said, "Yes, I am much better thanks to all of you being here and Mama's caretaking." Smoothing the pink blanket over her legs, she added, "And because we have made up our minds to tell you something important."

Her words were punctuated with another lightning flash and a loud clap of thunder. Serenity's and Sam's phones both pinged at the same time. They looked at each other and laughed. Of course they had set their phones the same way. Once again, Sam wondered why she had stayed away from her mom.

Lizzy looked at them both in alarm, but it was Sam who said that it was an alert, that the coming storm was almost there and would be a big one. Just then they heard two car doors slam.

"It's Tom and Brad," Mama said. "They would have closed the nursery a little early and come here knowing I have the generator that will keep the power on if the lights go out. This is good timing. We can tell all of you at the same time."

She got up to make another pot of coffee and put two frozen pizzas into the oven. A little comfort food would come in handy. By the time Tom and Brad reached the front porch, the rain had started to come down in sheets, and a huge wind was whipping the rain against the window.

"Sam?" Tom said to the woman waiting at the door for them. "I can't believe how grown up you are, and beautiful too," he added as he hugged her. "Have you met my husband? This is Brad."

Brad stuck out his hand to shake, but Sam pulled him into a hug instead. Brad looked at Serenity over Sam's head and she could see tears in his eyes. She knew why. Because at that moment, she saw Brad's memory of a similar introduction. It was when he introduced Tom to his brother and was pushed against the wall instead. Her eyes filled with tears in turn. *People can be so cruel when they are afraid*, she thought.

"I'll go help Mama," she said, giving Sam alone time with her grandmother and a chance to get to know Brad a little and to reacquaint herself with Tom. She had been a teenager when she had last seen him. Serenity loved Mama's kitchen. It looked the same as it did when she was a little girl and playing at Mama's house with Tom. It was a homey farm kitchen. A big sink sat in the middle of long counters.

A huge wooden island with stools around it took up the center of the kitchen. The island had been in the Tate's family for generations. She remembered sitting there as a kid, watching

Tom's dad make them pancakes. Mama had updated all the appliances, and the union of very modern and very old was perfect.

Serenity took a deep breath before saying, "I have something to tell you before I tell my mom."

Mama put down the stack of white plates she had in her hands and turned to her.

"I'm almost afraid to hear this," she said.

"I don't think it's a bad thing. But you will know."

Serenity paused, looked down, and sighed, and she said, "I met my father today, and he wants to see Lizzy."

Mama put her hand on her heart, and her face turned almost as white as the plates.

"Are you alright?" Serenity asked, taking her hand.

"My prayers have been answered," Mama said, using the plaid dish towel in her hand to wipe her eyes. She didn't want to tell Serenity how many times she had begged Lizzy not to send Matthew away. "How did this happen?"

As Serenity told her what she knew, Mama reached into the freezer and took out another pizza.

Seeing Serenity's puzzled look, Mama said. "I am going to have Brad call Randy and have him bring both men over here. You go tell your mom that the love of her life has come looking for her, and I am going to prepare myself to see John Carver."

Serenity didn't know what John Carver had to do with Mama, and even though Mama told her to tell her mom about Matthew, she was worried. Still, she knew enough to do what she was told and headed into the living room to break the news to her mother. Even if she really wasn't sure how Lizzy would react, it had to be done.

Everyone turned to look at her as she returned from the kitchen. She nodded at Sam and headed over to sit on the couch next to her mother's chair. Sam kneeled by the chair.

"What?" her mother asked. "What's wrong?"

In the kitchen, Mama held onto the edge of the sink and looked out at the storm lashing at the trees in the backyard. They bent and swayed with the wind but held strong. That was what she would have to do.

What Mama hadn't said to Serenity was what she hoped would happen. With everyone in the same room, they might figure out where Jimmy Hunter had gone. Because it seemed to her that everyone had come back to Lazy Rivers to figure it out. And that meant all the secrets needed to be told.

Forty Nine

Alex spent the rest of his day handling routine small-town issues, but his mind kept drifting back to his meeting with Serenity and the suspicious behavior of Betty Jean and Joseph. As evening approached, he took a more proactive approach. He drove to the diner, hoping to catch Betty Jean or Joseph before closing time. The storm that had popped up out of nowhere was now in full force, rain lashing against his windshield as he pulled up.

When he learned that Betty Jean and Joseph had both gone home, he decided to go see them despite the storm. He was tired of waiting for answers; he wanted them now. He knew where Betty Jean lived. It wasn't far, and he figured that's where Joseph had gone too. Why they thought no one knew about their relationship puzzled him. Maybe they just hoped they had kept it a secret. But they hadn't, and it was time to expose it.

And why a secret anyway, he thought as he drove through the rain, his windshield wipers beating furiously but hardly making a difference. Since it was hard to see, he was glad there weren't many people on the road, and that he wasn't going far, but one of the most dangerous parts of driving in a storm was that a tree might fall.

He had to risk it. Jimmy was out there somewhere, and he was positive Betty Jean and Joseph knew where he was, or if not that, at least knew more than they were telling. It had been almost a week since Jimmy had disappeared, and Alex knew all the statistics, but he was unwilling to accept them. Just as in his heart he was unwilling to accept that his brother Zach was dead. He had barely known him, but he did remember that it was Zach who protected him when his dad was angry.

And he remembered being angry too, at Zach when he was gone, even though he knew it wasn't Zach's fault that someone had taken him. That's what he had to tell himself, because otherwise, why would Zach leave him? His whole life had been driven towards finding out what had happened, and now it felt as if he might be close to discovery.

That he wanted to believe Zach was still alive somewhere probably made him an idiot, but he clung to the hope anyway that he'd see him someday. And not the way people always told him. Probably to make him feel better. That when he died, Zach would be waiting for him. That might be true. And it might not be.

Both versions were about hope, and Alex didn't see any difference in hoping he'd see Zach now in this life or possibly in another. Neither had any more proof than the other. And until he had that proof, he'd hope for what he wanted now.

Betty Jean's house had a small covered porch, so he was partially protected from the rain as he knocked on her door. He knew she knew he was there. And he figured she and Joseph were deciding what to do. It was Joseph who opened the door.

Well, I guess they decided what to do, Alex thought, as he walked in. Taking off his wet shoes, he put them on the tray that held shoes and hung his wet coat on the hooks above them and followed Joseph into the living room. Neither of them said anything.

Betty Jean was sitting in a chair by the fire, and she gestured to the other one across from her. Joseph settled into his chair. Still, no one spoke. Part of Alex wanted to leave this as it was. The room was warm and cozy. He thought how easy it would be to let it lull him into not asking questions. Just enjoy the company and the fire.

Finally, Betty Jean smiled at him and asked if he'd like coffee.

Alex shook his head. "That's kind of you, but right now perhaps we could just get to why I am here. I'm sure you know."

Joseph and Betty Jean exchanged a look, and Alex knew they were trying to decide what to say next and who would say it.

"I'm not sure we do," Joseph answered, as Betty Jean nodded.

Alex leaned forward in his chair, his arms on his knees, and looked at both of them in turn.

"I think you both do. The missing boys, the symbol Serenity saw, the strange connections between people who've suddenly returned to town. You two know something, and I need you to tell me what it is."

Betty Jean sighed, looked at Joseph and said, "Alex, it's not that simple."

"Make it simple," Alex insisted. "There's a boy missing right now, and I have a feeling this goes back further than just Jimmy. Maybe even back to my brother."

At the mention of Alex's brother, Joseph's expression changed. He looked at Betty Jean, who nodded almost imperceptibly.

"Alright," Joseph said, his voice low.

Just then, Alex's phone buzzed with a text from Serenity. "Big gathering at Mama Tate's. You need to be here."

Alex stared at the message, realizing that things were coming to a head faster than he'd anticipated. He texted back: "On my way. I'm bringing Betty Jean and Joseph, too."

Serenity's reply came quickly. "Yes. That's even better."

When Alex told Betty Jean and Joseph that they needed to come with him to Mama Tate's, Betty Jean sagged in her chair. It would have been so much easier to stay in her warm house and tell their story there than somewhere else.

But when Joseph helped her from her chair and said, "It will be better than a police station," she nodded in agreement.

Joseph said he'd drive the two of them to Mama's, and Alex agreed. He knew that neither of them liked what was happening, but they would do what they said they would do. In his heart he prayed they were not responsible for the boys going missing.

It would tear the town apart if they were charged with that crime. Betty Jean was a beloved figure in town, and although Joseph did his best to stay apart, he was still, like Big Mike before him, a symbol of the strength of Lazy Rivers.

As Alex drove towards Mama Tate's house, the storm raged around him. The wind pushed at his truck as if it was trying to push him off the road. He was glad that Joseph would drive Betty Jean in his truck. He was a good driver and he knew they'd be safe. At least physically safe.

And he hoped that what they ended up sharing kept them safe in other ways too. He hoped that all they had done wrong was keep a secret. However, he couldn't shake the feeling that by the end of the night, the landscape of Lazy Rivers—both literally and figuratively—would be forever changed.

At Mama Tate's, Serenity told Mama that three more people were coming and Mama went back into the kitchen to put another pizza in the oven. Before going she grabbed Serenity's arm. "Let's hope Matthew gets here first, and if he does, make sure Lizzy has had time to process seeing him before this turns into a circus."

Serenity knew just what she meant. So she texted Randy and told him to let Matthew come in before the two of them. He sent a thumbs up back. She looked at her mother. Lizzy hadn't said a word since she had told her that Matthew was coming. It was almost as if she was holding her breath, not sure how she felt.

The storm was so loud that they didn't hear the car pull up. It had started to hail along with the rain and the sound of the hail hitting the steel roof of the house was deafening. But Serenity was watching out the window and saw the car pull up and Matthew running for the door. She gestured to Sam, Tom, and Brad to go into the kitchen. Then she went to the door and let her father in, taking in his face once again, pointed to her mother, and left the room to the two of them.

At the kitchen door, she turned and looked back just in time to see Matthew help her mother out of the chair and hug her. For a moment her mother just stood there, and then her arms went around his neck.

In the kitchen, Mama Tate kept her back to the group pretending to be busy with dishes in the sink. She was afraid of what was going to come next. If John Carver was responsible for the missing boys, she didn't know how she could live with that.

$$Fifty$$

R andy and John watched Matthew run for the door and
duck inside, saying nothing to each other. They had parked
only a few feet away from the covered porch, but they knew
Matthew had been pelted with rain and hail and it would be their
turn next.

In the meantime, Randy kept the truck running to keep the
heater on. It had gone from a beautiful warm June day to a very
cold and wet one, and they needed the heat. Randy stopped the
windshield wipers, though. There was no point keeping them on.
They weren't going anywhere.

"How will we know when to go in?" John asked his son.

He only asked because he didn't know what else to say and
he was nervous. He really wasn't in a rush to go inside. Not just
because he didn't feel like facing what was coming next, but also
because he knew Matthew was seeing the woman he loved after

fifty years, and they obviously needed time together before what came next.

He had the same problem, except no one knew about it. Besides, he wasn't entirely sure it was the same thing. He and Ruth had each married someone else, and each of them had a son. It had been a good life for him, and as far as he could tell, it had been a good life for Ruth.

Now they were going to upset everything. Maybe things would get better, and maybe they would get worse. But at least the secret he had been carrying for years would be told, and no matter what happened after that, it would be a relief.

As he waited, John thought about all the times he had come to this house to see Ruth. He had loved being in the nursery, and Ted Tate seemed to love having him around. This place had always felt so welcoming. But would it be now?

"Don't know, dad," Randy answered. "But you seem really nervous about this whole thing. Do you have something you want to tell me first before we go in?"

That's the million-dollar question, John thought. *Do I? Should I?*

When his dad didn't answer, Randy started worrying. This was beginning to feel like an Agatha Christie novel where everyone gathers at the end and the killer is revealed. Is that what is going to happen here? Was the kidnapper going to be revealed, and his dad was part of it? *Impossible,* Randy said to himself, hoping that was true.

Inside the house, Brad, Tom, Mama, Serenity, and Sam were sitting around the wooden island, trying to pretend that everything was normal. Then the kitchen door opened, and Matthew and Lizzy came in, both of them looking flushed and happy.

"Let's eat," Lizzy said, breaking the tension. Everyone laughed and grabbed a slice of pizza. For the next few minutes, it felt as if nothing else was going on, except for a group of old friends reuniting.

Serenity put her arm around her daughter and Sam leaned in, making Serenity so happy she wanted to cry. Her daughter was home. Her father was home. Her mother was happy. What more could she want?

"Aren't we forgetting someone?" Tom said.

Seeing his mother blush and turn away, he wasn't sure if she was forgetting on purpose or just that so much else was going on. Brad took out his phone and texted Randy to come in, and the entire group went into the living room to greet them. Except Mama.

Tom looked back at his mother, standing alone in the kitchen, and came back in.

"What's happening?"

"Could you send John Carver in here?"

Tom didn't question why, although he wanted to. It felt eerily familiar to what had happened with Matthew and Lizzy. But John and his mother? He got to the living room just as the front door opened, bringing a gust of wind and a spatter of rain along with Randy and John. Even though they had gone only a few feet in the rain, they were soaking wet.

Tom helped them hang their wet coats on the hooks, joining the line of wet coats. But there were still more hooks. The house had been designed for gatherings, but until recently, it had felt empty when he visited. It certainly wasn't now.

As Randy and John headed into the living room, he was grateful to see that someone had brought the pizzas, plates, napkins, and drinks out to the massive coffee table.

"Help yourself," he gestured to Randy, but to John he said, "Mom wants to see you in the kitchen."

He wanted to ask more. Why would his mother want to see John alone? But he respected his mother's wishes and kept his thoughts to himself.

As he watched John walk to the kitchen, he realized John knew his way around the house. Of course he did. He and his mother had grown up together. That was probably all it was. Friends meeting after all these years.

For John, it was like going back in time. He knew this house as well as he knew his own. But still, he wasn't sure if Ruth's request scared him or delighted him. All he knew was that she was right.

They needed to talk first, even though he wasn't entirely sure what he would say.

Would he talk about his feelings that still lingered in the background or about what he knew about the missing boys? He still didn't know as he walked into the kitchen, the door swinging closed behind him.

But when he saw Ruth waiting for him, determination on her face, he understood he had no choice. It was time to tell her what he knew. But where to start? He was glad he hadn't had time to tell Randy before Tom called for them to come in. It was Ruth who needed to hear it first.

Ruth sighed, trying to decide what to do. But her instincts took over, and she walked to John and put her arms around him. At first, John hesitated. Would she still do this after he told her, but then he hugged her back. It was good enough for now.

Back at Betty Jean's house, Joseph helped Betty Jean into her raincoat and shrugged into his. His truck was in her garage, so they shouldn't get too wet. And he was sure he could drive through any storm. But it really wasn't the storm raging outside that felt dangerous. It was what they had to tell the group when they got to Mama's.

Joseph wrapped his arms around Betty Jean, and she leaned into him. He never tired of Betty Jean leaning into him. Even when he told her the family history, she still leaned in and said it was okay. He had never been so happy and grateful in his life, and that feeling had never gone away.

But now he was worried about what would happen once everyone heard the story. They might not be so forgiving. Especially Alex. Alex had a job to do, and Joseph knew he'd do it. But how he chose to do it would make all the difference.

Betty Jean leaned back and looked up at Joseph. "Maybe it's time to make that call." Inside she was yelling, *No, no, no,* but that wasn't the right response, and she knew it. It was time.

Joseph sighed and reached into his coat for his phone. He knew she was right, but the knowledge that after all this time, what they had done would be over, was almost more than he could handle. And he couldn't face her while he called. He walked into another room, silently closed the door, and dialed.

He closed his eyes as the phone rang. When it was answered, he didn't say anything. It wasn't needed. His hand shook as he held the phone, waiting for the man on the other end to speak.

"It's over, isn't it?" Zach said.

Fifty One

As Alex drove to the Tate house, he wondered if he had made the right decision. Maybe he should have forced Betty Jean and Joseph to come with him. But could he without resorting to force? And that could have resulted in injuries, and then what? This was his town; despite his life as a boy, he had always loved Lazy Rivers. Even the name made him happy. A river that meandered didn't try to be something it wasn't.

Right now he knew it was overflowing its banks, but once the storm was over, the river would return to being a slow-moving one that kept going up to Spring Falls, where it spilled into a ravine, and then continued to join other rivers and streams to make Silver Lake.

As he tried to see through the rain and hail pelting his truck, his headlights barely making a dent, he thought that the story of the boys going missing was doing the same thing. It had made its way through the town, getting larger each time a boy went missing, but then calming down again for years. Now he knew it had reached the tipping point.

All the pieces were falling into this river of time, and soon it would all make sense. It might not bring his brother back, but in his heart, he believed that Jimmy was still out there somewhere and they would find him. And all his answers lay ahead, just waiting for him to discover them.

The curtains were open at the Tate house so he could see all the people there as he pulled up in his truck, trying to get as close as possible to the front porch. It both embarrassed and worried him that in the middle of all of this, the person he was searching for was Serenity.

But when he saw her through the window, her red hair glowing, his heart beat a little harder. *Don't be stupid,* he said to himself. *She's not interested in you; we are just solving this mystery together.* It didn't help that he had that same feeling for her when he was a boy. But back then, being five years older was a big deal. And besides, he was busy then just trying to survive his father.

It was Serenity who opened the door for him and helped him out of his wet coat. A tremendous clap of thunder and a lightning flash happened at the same time, and the lights went out. For a moment, they stood together in the dark. He could feel her breath, and he reached out to touch her just as the generator kicked on and the lights returned.

She smiled at him; his heart thudded, but he was sure she did not know what he felt.

"Are Joseph and Betty Jean on their way?"

"They should be right behind me."

Serenity paused for a second and waited.

"Memory?"

Instead of answering, she just nodded and led him into the living room. A fresh pizza had been brought out, and everyone turned to say hello. For a minute it felt just like a gathering of old friends, even though he barely knew everyone, but then Alex remembered they had come together to figure out what had happened.

Serenity introduced him to Matthew and John and then pulled a chair for him into the circle around the coffee table. Tom, Brad, and Mama sat on one sofa. John, and Sam on the other. Randy stood behind the sofa as if he were guarding his father, *and maybe Sam*, Alex thought. Matthew stood beside Lizzy's chair, his hand on her shoulder, perhaps to reassure himself that she was actually there.

Serenity pulled up another chair for herself beside his but then stood instead. He looked up at her, and she shook her head. She needed to stand and move a little. There were so many memories in this room, it was becoming overwhelming.

She looked at her mother and daughter and saw that they were having the same problem. Both their eyes were glazed. This had never happened before, where there were so many memories that she couldn't sort out whose were whose.

But then, they had never let themselves be in a room with so many people, let alone people who were trying to solve a mystery. And at least one of them in the room knew something that they weren't telling about the missing boys.

And then she knew who it was. She looked at John Carver. He dropped his head and sighed. Mama reached out and held his hand.

"Go ahead, John, tell them what you know," Mama said softly.

Serenity took a seat and waited. John rolled up his shirt to show the scar on his left arm. "This used to be something else," he said. "A symbol."

"Like this one?" Serenity said, showing him the picture on her phone.

"Like that one," John said. His face was flushed, and Serenity thought he was close to tears. Randy looked at her as if pleading to not let this go on, but it had to. This was the beginning of the end. The room fell silent, all eyes on John. He took a deep breath, his hand trembling slightly as he traced the scar on his arm.

"It started fifty years ago," John began, his voice barely above a whisper. "We were just kids, really, following Big Mike. You know how Big Mike was. He said follow, and you did. Me and Zach."

Alex tensed at the mention of his brother's name and wanted to say something, but Serenity touched his arm, and he stilled.

John continued, "We thought we were doing something good, protecting the town. Big Mike told us about ancient symbols, secret societies. Said we could be part of something bigger."

He paused, looking around the room. The faces staring back at him were a mix of confusion, concern, and growing horror.

"We were stupid kids. We believed him. We adopted the symbol and swore an oath. But then... he started talking about sacrifices. About how the town needed to give something to stay protected."

Serenity felt her stomach drop. She could see the memory playing out in John's mind and could feel the fear and regret washing over him.

"Zach was the first to say no," John said, looking directly at Alex. "And then he disappeared."

Alex stood up abruptly, his face pale. "Are you saying... are you saying you had something to do with my brother's disappearance?"

John shook his head vehemently. "No! We didn't... we didn't do anything to Zach. But I think Big Mike did, and Joseph knew about it and never told. I was too afraid to confront him, so I left town."

The room erupted in a chorus of shocked gasps and angry outbursts. Serenity raised her hands, trying to calm everyone down.

"John," she said, her voice steady despite the turmoil in her mind. "What about the other boys? Jimmy?"

John's shoulders slumped. "I thought it was over after Zach. We tried to forget, to move on. But every few decades, I heard a boy would go missing."

Just then, the front door burst open. Joseph and Betty Jean stumbled in, soaked from the rain. Joseph was stoic as always, Betty Jean in tears.

"It's over," he said, his voice hoarse. "I just got off the phone with Zach. He's alive. And he knows where Jimmy is."

The room fell silent once more, the weight of this revelation settling over everyone. The storm outside seemed to crescendo, a particularly loud thunderclap punctuating Joseph's words. Serenity looked around the room at the shocked faces of her family and friends. She reached down and put her hand on Alex's shoulder. His head was dropped, and he was trembling.

What would it feel like to know your brother was alive after all these years? What did it mean? How could Zach know where Jimmy was? Did he take him? Why? Where were the other boys?

As the rain continued to pour outside, Serenity knew that Lazy Rivers would never be the same after tonight. The river of secrets had finally reached its falls, and now they all had to face the consequences of what lay at the bottom.

Fifty Two

Zach put the phone down and turned to look at the boy sitting on the other bed watching a show on the iPad he had bought him.

The thunder outside was so loud the vibrations shook the cheap motel room they were in. Lightning lit up the curtains with flowers on them, so faded they were barely there. They looked like the same curtains from the last time he was in this motel. When he was a boy. With Big Mike.

He couldn't believe it was over. After all this time. He looked down at his left arm, at the symbol there, and sighed. Somehow it had been put on upside down on his arm, and he had always wondered if that meant what he had agreed to do had been wrong. Upside down.

But Big Mike had been so convincing. And Zach had been so unhappy. Not just unhappy. Afraid. Even after all these years, he still could feel the fear of running and hiding from a man with a stick or a belt. If he hid well enough and his father couldn't find him, sometimes his father would fall asleep in a drunken stupor and not even remember that he had been angry when he woke up. Except sometimes he would be even angrier.

His brothers left, one at a time, as soon as they were old enough to get away. His sister somehow escaped the worst of it. Maybe his father had some values left. But each time a brother left, he became more of a target. At least he could protect his little brother, Alex, by directing his father's anger away from Alex and onto him.

And then one day after he turned ten, Big Mike came to see him. He told Zach he knew what his father had been doing to his children. And if Zach wanted, he could take him away from it all.

It took a couple of visits to convince Zach. He wanted to leave, but he was worried about his little brother. Big Mike promised to look after him, and when Alex got old enough, if he wanted to leave, he'd take him away too. That was Big Mike's rule. Boys had to be old enough to make the decision themselves. Then he would help them "run away" and find a new life. Sometimes with another family, sometimes in the group home they kept together.

But then Big Mike died, and Zach was the one left to take care of the boys, along with Joseph. And it was Joseph who watched over Alex, even though it didn't seem much like watching over. But Joseph said Alex could handle it, and Zach guessed he had because, look at him now, the sheriff. Whether that was good or bad for him remained to be seen.

After Joseph took over, it wasn't the same, though. Big Mike had expanded his outreach to other towns, and Joseph only agreed to watch over the boys in Lazy Rivers. He had never fully embraced his father's idea that saving boys in trouble was the right thing to do—someone in the family who loved the boy having to sacrifice having them in their life. Like him leaving Alex behind.

Once in a while Joseph had brought Zach boys from town, including Jimmy. Well, Joseph didn't bring them; he helped Zach talk to them, made sure they were ready and willing, and then Zach did everything else.

After Joseph and Betty Jean got together, Joseph told her. She tried to talk him out of continuing, but he had promised his father, and that was that. So she helped by setting it up so that most of the profit from Joseph's side business supported their little program.

It paid Zach enough to watch over boys in the home until they had a new one and to take care of the ones that stayed. Sometimes, boys wanted to go back to their real homes, and the only caveat was that they could never tell where they had been. They had all agreed, understanding the danger they would put their friends in if they did.

Zach knew some of the boys kept in touch and remained friends as adults. He had been proud of what he and Joseph had done. But all along, it worried him that sometimes the parents weren't quite as bad as the boys had claimed. And Jimmy was one of them. He had already decided to take Jimmy back home when Joseph called. And they had already agreed to shut the program down after Jimmy.

There were no boys left at the home. Jimmy was the last one. The house had been cleared and put up for sale. The proceeds would go to Alex. Maybe he would start some kind of trust with it. And there was something else that he didn't tell Joseph. Something that would keep him from doing this much longer.

All he had told Joseph was he was getting too old for this. And that was true. Taking care of the boys had been his entire life, and now he wanted to go spend the rest of his life, no matter how short, with his brother. But would Alex forgive him? Would the town forgive him? Would he go to jail along with Joseph and maybe Betty Jean because she had helped too?

It was for those reasons he had first decided to return Jimmy and then run away himself to keep everyone else safe. But now it was too late. John Carver was going to tell. He knew because John had called and told him. So he was prepared for what was happening when Joseph called.

Until then, he and Jimmy had been staying at a motel in Spring Falls, making sure that leaving was what Jimmy wanted. Now they were in a tiny motel outside Lazy Rivers. It wasn't a nice place, and he would be glad to be out of it. On the other hand, it was probably nicer than a jail cell.

He had washed Jimmy's clothes so that he could go home wearing the clothes he had been wearing when he left. Jimmy had cried most of the week. He missed his mom and his sister. This was the right thing to do.

This time, though, instead of simply dropping Jimmy off at his house, he would take him in himself. Whatever happened after that, he'd have to deal with. It had been his life choice, right or wrong. He couldn't blame anyone else for it.

"It's time," he said to Jimmy. Jimmy's eyes lit up. He put the iPad into the backpack Zach had given him and stood by the bed, waiting, trembling a little, but doing his best to hide it.

Taking one last look in the mirror, Zach wondered if anyone would know him now. The only thing the same about him was he was still short for a man and his eyes were still brown. The spiky blond hair was long gone.

"I'm afraid they'll be mad at me," Jimmy said.

"No, son, they will be overjoyed to see you. They will be mad at me."

He looked down at the symbol on his arm of what he had been doing with his life, rolled his sleeves down, shrugged into an old sweater, picked up his suitcase, and turned out the hotel room lights, leaving the key on the dresser. Then, holding his raincoat over Jimmy's head, the two of them stepped out into the storm.

Jimmy was going home to people that loved him. Zach didn't think that would be the same for him, but he was going anyway.

Fifty Three

A few months later...

Serenity walked quickly, sometimes jogging, in a hurry to get home. It was amazing how fast her strength had returned, and now walking every morning was so much easier, and she looked forward to it. Each day, she saw something she had never seen before.

A lone truck passed her, and she saw Pete at the wheel. She waved, thinking how wonderful it was not to cringe when someone saw her. Seeing memories was still hard, but she was getting used to it. This time, a memory of Pete and his wife went by and disappeared as his truck took the turn in the road. It was a good one, and she smiled. It was a gift to be let into someone's life like that.

The August morning was already warm, and she knew it would get much hotter, but for now, the sun hid behind white and pink cotton-candy clouds, only breaking through occasionally to send golden shafts of light onto the road.

As she walked, Serenity let herself drift back to the night of the storm and its aftermath. Only a few minutes after Joseph and Betty Jean arrived, Alex had gotten a call telling him that Jimmy had come home along with Zach.

He had turned to her, eyes filled with tears, and asked her to come with him. That had surprised her, but she had said yes. If he needed her, she would be there.

The storm had stopped almost at the same moment that Joseph and Betty Jean had arrived, so when they stepped outside, the rain clouds had moved away and the full moon shone high in the sky. The moonlight revealed the damage the storm had done; there were tree limbs everywhere, but it also glinted off the puddles and drops of water on the leaves, making it a fairyland of sparkles.

It was the same contrast she had felt about Jimmy returning. It was over. That was wonderful. But there was damage that needed to be repaired.

Alex had told everyone to go home; he'd talk to them later. And he reminded Joseph and Betty Jean not to leave town. As they drove away, she had turned in her seat to see everyone surround Joseph and Betty Jean, patting them on the back and hugging. No matter what they had done, they had meant to do well.

At the Hunter's house, the two reunions were almost too much for her. The family had wept at Jimmy's return and even hugged

Zach for bringing him back. Perhaps forgetting that he was the one who took him away.

But the hardest part was that so many of Zach's and Alex's memories had crashed into her head at once that she had to turn away. But instead of running, she had stood and let them wash in and out, and then all that remained was their joy at seeing each other again.

Two months later, not everything was settled yet. Technically, the three of them had committed a crime. It was up to the courts to decide what to do with them, but the town itself as a whole was not wanting them punished. So they were all pushing for some sort of community service and probation.

In a way, that was perfect since they had believed that they had been doing community service, and keeping it secret had been a form of probation. Serenity had to trust that kindness would win the day with the three of them. Besides, Zach wasn't well. He probably wouldn't last long in jail.

As she walked up the no-longer rutted road to the house, she could see Sam waiting for her on the large front porch that had been added to the house. It spanned the entire house so that whether they wanted to watch the sunrise or sunset, they had a place to sit. It had been Randy's idea. It cost a lot, but she thought it was worth it. She wasn't planning to go anywhere, and she had savings that were waiting for something special to do with them. And this was special.

The inside of the house was almost finished. Just a few things needed to be done in the kitchen, and they had added an extra bathroom, so they all had one. That too seemed an excess at first, but Lizzy had insisted on it. Serenity understood why. Lizzy didn't want there to be any reason her girls, as she now called them, wouldn't stay.

Now that her studio was done, she had started painting again, and Sam had set up a room for herself to write, although Sam was often off writing at the diner, where she said she liked the background noise. Serenity thought there were more reasons than that. She knew Randy often dropped by.

Since Matthew had returned, her mother had gotten better. She still wasn't sure that Lizzy hadn't made herself sick in the first place so that they would come home. For whatever reason, they had all returned. Sam, Serenity, John, Matthew, Zach, and little Jimmy.

As she reached the porch, Sam handed her a steaming mug of coffee and leaned against the porch railing, looking very much at home. Behind her, Serenity could hear the low murmur of voices from inside the house. Her mother, Lizzy, was in deep conversation with Matthew. They had a lot of catching up to do, but the smiles on their faces whenever they looked at each other told Serenity that they were on the right path.

"So," Sam said, "what happens now?"

Serenity took a sip of her coffee, savoring the warmth. She knew what Sam was asking. "Now? Now we heal. We move forward."

As if on cue, Alex's police cruiser pulled up to the house. He stepped out, and even from a distance, Serenity could see the relief written across his face. He looked years younger now that his brother and Jimmy were home. Zach was in the passenger seat, looking older and wearier than Serenity had imagined, but alive. And that was also why Alex looked relieved. Zach was getting treated for his cancer instead of just giving up.

"I still can't believe it," Sam murmured. "All those years, and he was just trying to help in his own misguided way."

Serenity nodded. "Sometimes the right intentions can lead us down the wrong path. But what matters is that we find our way back."

They watched as Alex helped Zach out of the car. The two brothers stood for a moment, just looking at each other, before Alex pulled Zach into a tight embrace.

"Mom," Sam said softly, "I'm glad I came back. I'm glad we're facing this together."

Serenity felt her heart swell with emotion. She put an arm around her daughter's shoulders and pulled her close. There were no words to tell her how happy she was, but she thought Sam could feel it.

As Alex and Zach made their way up the path, Sam told Serenity that she had seen Joseph and Betty Jean at the diner. "They looked tired but relieved," she said, "the weight of their secret finally lifted. Whatever happens next, at least they know they aren't alone."

"It's not going to be easy," Serenity said, more to herself than to Sam. "There's still a lot to work through, a lot of healing to do."

Sam nodded. "But we'll do it together, right? All of us?"

"All of us," Serenity agreed.

She thought about the symbol, about the memories she'd seen, about the pain and the secrets that had shaped Lazy Rivers for so long. But she also thought about the strength she'd seen in her family, in her friends, in this town. As Alex reached the porch, his eyes met Serenity's, and she felt a flutter in her chest. There was so much to look forward to, so many new memories to make. Memories she wouldn't be so afraid of seeing in the future.

"Welcome home," she said, and she meant it for all of them—for Zach, for Sam, for herself. The town had weathered its storm, and though there would undoubtedly be more challenges ahead, Serenity knew they would face them together.

After all, that's what families do, she thought. And Lazy Rivers, with all its flaws and all its beauty, was one big, complicated, wonderful family.

As they all filed into the house, the sound of laughter and conversation spilling out onto the porch, Serenity stood for a moment on her own. Nearby, she could hear the soft flow of the river. And like time, it just kept moving on.

And like time, it always brought the promise of new beginnings, Serenity thought. It was up to them what to do with that promise.

And for the first time in a long time, Serenity felt truly at peace. She knew that whatever waited around the corner, she wouldn't be dealing with it alone.

Acknowledgements

I could never write a book without the help of friends and family support. But for many years, both Jet Tucker and Diana Cormier have taken the time to do the final reader proof, and Laura Moliter provides fantastic book editing. I can always trust that they will tell me what I might have missed in my books. Which gives me peace of mind, which is worth its weight in gold.

And a thank you to all the people who tell me they love to read these stories. Comments from friends and strangers are more valuable than gold.

And as always, thank you to my beloved husband, Del, for being my daily sounding board, for putting up with all my questions, for my constant need to want to make things better, and for being the love of my life in more than just this one lifetime.

Author Notes

The concept that time is simply a series of memories fascinates me. And that those memories are not accurate and we can rewrite them makes it even more interesting.

That, along with the awareness that many of us are stuck in the memories or stories that keep us from being in the present moment, as well as my love of the strength and resilience of strong women, caused a story to emerge for me.

I chose the river as a metaphor for life because it is constantly in flux, never remaining the same, and as we learn to flow with it, life becomes richer.

I also wanted to explore the idea that we are often afraid of our gifts, and instead of using them, we run, hide, or deny them.

So although this story revolves around the mystery of the missing boys, it is really about missing people. Both in their own lives and in the lives of others.

What happens next? There is another mystery to be solved. This time from Lizzy's past. I hope you'll join me as we continue to travel the Rivers of Time together.

If you have read *The Ruby Sisters* series or the single book *Follow Me Here*, you probably recognized the characters living in Spring Falls. If you haven't read them, I hope you'll try them, too.

All my books live in the same "universe" of small towns, only a few hours away from each other.

Strong women, friendships, community, and possibilities that lie beyond the five senses are themes in all my fiction books. You can find all of them at your favorite bookstore or library.

If you liked this book, I'd be so grateful if you'd spread the word. And I'd love to have you join my newsletter. (https://geni.us/subscribe-booklink)

Also By Beca

The Rivers of Time Series: Women's Lit, Friendship, Small Town, Mystery, Magical Realism, Small Town Fiction
The Returning, The Awakening, The Rising

Follow Me Here: **Women's Lit, Friendship, Small Town, Mystery, Magical Realism, Small Town Fiction**

The Ruby Sisters Series: Women's Lit, Friendship, Mystery, Small Town Fiction
A Last Gift, After All This Time, And Then She Remembered, As If It Was Real, Almost Innocent

Stories From Doveland: Women's Lit, Friendship, Small Town, Mystery, Magical Realism, Small Town Fiction

Karass, Pragma, Jatismar, Exousia, Stemma, Paragnosis,
In-Between, Missing, Out Of Nowhere

The Return To Erda Series: Fantasy
Shatterskin, Deadsweep, Abbadon, The Experiment

The Chronicles of Thamon: Fantasy
Banished, Betrayed, Discovered, Wren's Story

The Shift Series: Spiritual Self-Help
Living in Grace: The Shift to Spiritual Perception
The Daily Shift: Daily Lessons From Love To Money
The 4 Essential Questions: Choosing Spiritually Healthy Habits
The 28 Day Shift To Wealth: A Daily Prosperity Plan
The Intent Course: Say Yes To What Moves You
Imagination Mastery: A Workbook For Shifting Your Reality
Right Thinking: A Thoughtful System for Healing
Perception Mastery: Seven Steps To Lasting Change
Blooming Your Life: How To Experience Consistent Happiness

Perception Parables: Very short stories
Love's Silent Sweet Secret: A Fable About Love
Golden Chains And Silver Cords: A Fable About Letting Go

Advice / Journals

*A Woman's ABC's of Life: Lessons in Love, Life, and Career from
Those Who Learned The Hard Way*

The Daily Nudge(s): So When Did You First Notice

About Beca

Beca writes books she hopes will change people's perceptions of themselves and the world, and open possibilities to things and ideas that are waiting to be seen and experienced.

At sixteen, Beca founded her own dance studio. Later, she received a Master's Degree in Dance in Choreography from UCLA and founded the Harbinger Dance Theatre, a multimedia dance company, while continuing to run her dance school.

After graduating—to better support her three children—Beca switched to the sales field, where she worked as an employee and independent contractor in many industries, excelling in each while perfecting and teaching her Shift System and writing books.

She joined the financial industry in 1983 and became an Associate Vice President of Investments at a major stock brokerage firm. She was a licensed Certified Financial Planner for over twenty years.

This diversity, along with a variety of life challenges, helped fuel the desire to share what she's learned by writing and speaking, hoping it will make a difference in other people's lives.

Beca grew up in State College, PA, with the dream of becoming a dancer and then a writer. She carried that dream forward as she fulfilled a childhood wish by moving to Southern California in 1968. Beca told her family she would never move back to the cold.

After living there for thirty-one years, she met her husband, Delbert Lee Piper, Sr., at a retreat in Virginia, and everything changed. They decided to find a place they could call their own, which sent them off traveling around the United States. They lived and worked in a few different places before returning to live in the cold once again near Del's family in a small town in Northeast Ohio, not too far from State College.

When not working and teaching together, they love to visit and play with their combined family of eight children and five grandchildren, walk, read, study, do yoga or taiji, feed birds, and work in their garden.